Bloody Eden

T.L. Knighton

DEDICATION

To Kimberly

We who are left behind are richer for having known you,
and poorer for having lost you.

ACKNOWLEDGMENTS

This book would not be here without the love and support of my loving family. In particular, my wife Jennifer who has managed to put up with many countless hours with me blasting music in my ears so I could work, despite being just a few feet away from her. Also, my son Robby, who thinks every story I come up with is absolute gold. While that's not true, it's nice to hear. In addition, I must thank my mother and editor, Bonnie Jefferson, who has given me support since before I entered this world.

I'd also like to thank a couple of my fellow authors. First, Cedar Sanderson, who helped out in many ways, including providing the photograph used to make the cover of this book.

Also, I have to thank Sarah A. Hoyt, who nudged me into publishing a novelette to see if anyone would like my writing. That novelette was "After the Blast", which lead directly to this book. The response to "Blast" was tremendous, and I owe it to Sarah and her blog's readers. Thanks folks.

<u>Chapter 1</u>

A young woman, her blonde hair dirty and greasy, cowered in the stained corner. The room stank of human waste. She muttered a prayer, barely audible, for the family recently thrown into her own personal hell.

The man, woman, and boy had been beaten, their facial features masked beneath the bruises and cuts. She could only tell that they had dark hair and dark eyes. Their barely conscious bodies piled in the center of the room, what had once been a living room in a suburban home. Dark stains covered the once white walls.

Two men, one short and thin while the other was a full head taller and heavily muscled, stood looking down at the three. Malevolence gleamed in their eyes.

The thin man cackled, his yellowed teeth dotting his open mouth. "Come on Earl. Lemme cut 'em this time?"

Earl snarled at the newcomers huddled together, the man wrapping his arm around the woman and child, his embrace a shield that would protect them.

"Come on, Earl. You got to cut the last two."

Earl slammed the back of his hand into the other man's jaw, snapping his head back.

"Ow! Whatcha do that for?" the thin man whined.

"I can't think with you jawin' in my damn ear."

The thin man rubbed his jaw. "Ya coulda just said somethin'."

Earl looked at the family huddled in the floor and smiled ominously. "You're just gonna have to forgive my brother. He gets a bit excitable come supper time."

The man looked at the woman and child, then back at Earl. "You don't mean…?"

"I do," Earl said. "But you shouldn't fret none. Some of us have to die so that others may live and all that."

"You're sick," the woman barked, he flaming red hair a harbinger of her spirit.

Earl slammed the back of his hand against her cheek, her head snapping around. "No, we're not. We're alive. That's a damn sight better than most folks we knew from back when, now ain't it?"

The big man pulled out a large knife, wiping it menacingly across his sleeve.

A whimper sounded from the corner. Earl shifted his gazed toward the blonde. "I'll be with you in a minute. Now shut the hell up and let me work."

Earl turned back toward the family. "Now, where was I?" His lips started to curl into an evil grin and instant before the front of his head exploded.

The family jumped as they found themselves coated in blood.

The front door crashed down, bodies pouring in, each armed with rifles. Gunshots echoes against the walls as the thin man jerked from the rounds punching into his body before finally falling onto the hardwood floor.

The invaders filtered throughout the house. From time to time, one would call out, "Clear!"

One of the men, shorter than most of the others with salt and pepper hair and thin like most people these days, knelt before the family. His dark red shirt and dusty brown pants contrasted against the pooling blood on the floor. On his hip was a leather gun belt with knife sheath that looked like it belonged in the Old West, except for the dulled nickel semi-automatic pistol resting in the holster. The knife was also a modern style looking slightly odd in the old timey rig. "You're alright. We won't hurt you," he said in a soothing voice. "I'm going to get you some medical attention, alright?"

The man nodded.

The kneeling man turned his head, yelling

over his shoulder, "Hector!"

A large Latino man, probably in his mid thirties, ran through the busted door. "Yeah, boss?"

"Can you check these folks out? Make sure they're good to go?"

Hector nodded. "Can do."

The man in charge stood up and looked toward the girl in the corner. "We're gonna need you over there next."

Hector nodded while poking and prodding the family.

The other man walked toward the girl. "Like I said to them, no one's going to hurt you, alright?"

The girl tried to pull more into herself, as if willing her body to shrink.

Recognition seemed to dawn in the man's eyes. "Katie? Katie Miller?"

The girl jumped at the mention of her own name. He knelt down and craned his neck, trying to put his face in her line of sight. "Katie, it's me. It's Jason. Jason Calvin."

She turned her head to look at his face, still not meeting his gaze. "M...mister Jason?" she asked, the pain of speaking distorting her words.

Jason smiled softly. "Yep, it's me. We've been worried about you for a while now. You alright?"

Katie shook her head. "I didn't want to. None of it. I know I can't help what they did to me. That ain't my fault. I know that. But the other..."

Jason gently touched her shoulder. "We know that, darlin'. We all know that. I don't suspect they gave you a whole lot of choice. No one here's going to judge you, alright?"

He stood and grabbed a man passing by. "Get these chains off of her as quick as you can, got it?"

The man nodded and ran off as ordered.

** ** **

Jason helped the woman, who'd introduced herself as Megan Hernandez, into the wagon. It wasn't much, just the back end of a pickup truck modified to be pulled by a horse and a bench up front for the driver, like most wagons these days, but it didn't involve walking. Her husband, Mark, and their son Xander followed.

Katie, the blonde girl, was cowering in the front corner of the wagon. Her eyes darted around the overgrown suburb like a caged animal.

"I'm sorry for the lack of comfort," Jason said with a soft smile.

"We're not really in any position to

complain, Mr. Calvin," Mark said.

Jason shook his head. "It's just Jason, okay?"

Mark nodded. "Jason. Got it."

"Excuse me, Jason?" Megan asked.

Jason raised his eyebrows in answer.

"We're appreciative, you've got to know that," she said.

"But?" Jason heard this thing before, and was ready.

"What's going to happen to us?"

"To start with, we're going to get you all some food. Fill your bellies. Then we're going to talk to you a bit, find out what you do or did, and most likely ask you to stick around."

Megan took a deep breath, her face troubled. "And if we say no?"

This was the part that Jason enjoyed. "Then we try to outfit you as best we can so you'll be as safe as possible on your way," he said. "We don't keep anyone against their will. We aren't those kind of folks."

Jason looked at Katie. He could barely imagine what all she'd been through, but figured it would be years before the smiling face he thought of as hers would show itself again. "If Katie decides to talk, she can tell you a bit about it," he said, adding, "but I wouldn't push it. As bad as you folks had it, I think she may have

11

had it worse."

Both adults nodded. Hector declared them all fit for travel physically, though Katie was less than fit psychologically. Jason decided to load her up anyways. He didn't figure sitting around the house of horrors would be any better.

Jason, not being a horseman, finally mounted up on a brown horse on the third try. "I'll ride right beside you folks, so if you've got any questions or anything, you just ask."

The couple nodded as Xander's eyes drank in the surrounding sights. The wagon bumped down what had once been a highway, now overgrown with weeds. Abandoned cars, now nothing more than rusting hulks, littered the sides of the road and the median.

"Everywhere else, the cars are in the road," Mark commented. "Folks in Tennessee just more polite in the face of a nuclear war of something?"

Jason chuckled. "Not quite. This is New Eden territory, technically. One of our projects has been to clear the roads. They pushed them out of the way so the roads can actually be used."

"New Eden?"

"Home," he said with a warm smile.

The hours dragged on as the group, five men plus the recently freed prisoners, pushed on down the abandoned highway. Jason made small talk with the family as best he could. They admitted they were originally from Texas, but had headed out of there shortly after seeing a mushroom cloud over Dallas while out driving.

He figured they didn't want to tell him anything, but Jason was used to that. While years of what he had always described as office work was a liability immediately after the blast, Jason Calvin had been a pretty good journalist. He knew how to draw information out of people.

Before they realized what they were saying, they were answering his questions and filling in most of the blanks. The couple flatly refused to talk about the last several months though, and Jason decided it best not to push.

The road circled around one of the many mountains until a small settlement became visible in the valley below. Even from up here, the hustle and bustle was obvious.

"That," Jason said, pausing dramatically, "Is New Eden."

The highway snaked its way down the mountains, switching back and forth as it worked its way down into the valley. As they approached the settlement, the outline of houses became clearer, revealing their unusual construction.

13

"What are they made of?" Megan asked.

"Old fashioned wattle and daub mostly," Jason answered. "A few are a little different. My place is cob."

"Huh?"

"Basically, it's mud slapped on a woven frame shaped like a house. Then we roof it with whatever we can manage. Cob is a little different. It's like building with adobe, only you skip making bricks and just build the wall straight up."

"Do either of 'em work?"

Jason shrugged. "About as well as anything else we've thought of. What I'd give for central air though."

Megan's eyes widened momentarily before returning to normal, then nodded. *Odd. Something there. Might need to poke around a little later and see if they'll talk more,* he thought.

The group wove their way through a maze of haphazardly placed homes, all of different shape, along the dusty road. As they went, Jason commented on the person who lived in that home, or how that was actually a shop where one could get whatever.

They stopped in a large open square in the middle of town. People filtered in from every direction.

Jason looked at one of the townspeople, a

man in heavily worn jeans and an old ratty t-shirt. "Go get Marlene Miller."

The man nodded and ran off at a full sprint.

Several people came over to the wagon and reached out to help the family down, hunks of bread soon thrust into their hands.

Jason looked around, scanning the crowd for one particular head. His head swiveled back and forth several times before the flash of red hair. He focused in, finally seeing one of the faces that mattered most in his life.

He dismounted and immediately made his way through the crowd until the rest of the redhead was visible. "About time you got home," she said, her wide smile showing off her perfect teeth.

He looked into her deep blue eyes. "Sorry, traffic was a bitch," Jason answered with a smile of his own as he took the redhead in an embrace.

He loved Jess with all his heart. He still didn't know why she married him, but she did and he was thrilled. He also understood why a would-be warlord wanted her. Of course, it had turned out to be a big mistake for the warlord.

"How bad?" she asked.

"Bad. Katie Miller was there too, chained up in a corner."

Jess closed her as she turned her head for a moment. "Did she...?"

Jason nodded.

"Oh, God," she whispered.

"She didn't have much of a choice."

Jess looked up and smiled. "I know. It's not that. John Baskin's been stirring up some crap."

He rolled his eyes. "What the hell now?"

"The usual."

From behind, Jason heard a shrill voice screaming. "Be gone, foul demon!"

Jason sighed as he turned and walked toward the voice.

Standing a few feet from the wagon stood a tiny man with a weasel-like face, dressed in black clothes, all in varying degrees of fade. In his hand was a homemade wooden cross, the cross-piece slightly askew.

"Back off, Baskin," Jason called out.

"I'll do no such thing," the man in black barked. "You brought a demon into our midst. She has feasted on the flesh of her fellow man and must be cleansed by fire." With that, Baskin held up a gas can. Gas sloshed within.

Jason's hand rested on the pistol strapped to his hip.

Baskin's eyes widened. "You would shoot a man of God?"

"Not any God I know." Jason's demeanor

turned ice cold as his hand came to rest on the pistol's grip.

"John Baskin!" called out a familiar voice. Jason instantly relaxed slightly but kept his hand ready on the pistol.

"This don't concern you none," Baskin said, holding his hand out as if to keep the new arrival away.

"You're using that 'man of God' stuff again, even though you ain't been ordained by anyone. That does concern me. I'm kind of responsible for everyone here's immortal soul, after all," the new man said.

Jason looked sideways at Reverend Michael Hardesty. Hardesty was a good and Godly man and all that, but he was also practical. The man was a fighter. He had a body count behind him. The Good Lord may have said to turn the other cheek, but Hardesty knew enough to know that Christ had also instructed his followers to buy a sword if they didn't have one. Hardesty had used *his* sword more than once.

"I am a man of God, more than you, who allow fornicators and demons in this town," Baskin said, his hands quivering with every word.

"Thou shalt not kill. Remember that one?" Hardesty fired back.

"I am purging this community, purifying it

against the demonic forces that lead us to this low point in human history."

Jason looked at Hardesty. "He always talk like this?"

Hardesty shrugged. "Radiation does some weird things, after all, but nah, this is new. Thinks God spared him to force mankind to repent of our evil ways. He means to purge the evildoers and such."

Jason turned his gaze back on Baskin. "I'll tell you what, John. You even think of 'purging' a single person in this here community, and I'll purge this here pistol of the 124 grain hollow points it's carrying. Understood?"

"You won't do it. You don't have the guts," Baskin said, a smug grin crossing his face.

Jason smiled coldly. "Try me." His fingers gently tightened around the CZ-75B's grip.

"Knock it off, Baskin. This is your last warning," said Simon Redfeather, who served as town council chairman of New Eden, as he walked into the square. "Next time, you're out."

"God's will-"

"Oh shut the Hell up about God's will. You don't know it any better than you know how to build a nuclear reactor," Simon said, walking up to Jason. "About time you got back."

Jason released his grip on the pistol and took an offered hand. "Tell me about it."

"Done?"

"Yeah. Left 'em hung up on the highway as a warning."

Simon nodded, then turned his attention back to Baskin. "You're still here?"

The weasel looking man turned and stormed off.

"Looks like things haven't exactly been quiet while I've been gone," Jason said.

"Baskin means well and all that, but he's crossing lines he doesn't even know he's crossing," Hardesty said.

Simon nodded. "Yeah, and he really is an idiot to boot. It probably would have been a mercy to have let you pop him."

Jason chuckled. "I don't think killing him will put him out of his misery. I suspect it'll keep going on afterward."

"Who said anything about ending his suffering? I was talking about ours!" Simon said with a laugh.

"Tempting in so many ways," Jason said, smiling. "So, besides Baskin and his crap, what did I miss?"

"Other than that, not much," Simon said. "Pretty quiet otherwise."

"Great. I'm going to end up being out of a job if I'm not careful," he said with a smile.

Simon returned it. "Nah. We'll just make up

more laws until you've got something to do."

Jason rolled his eyes. "Great. In that case, let me quit now."

Simon laughed. "What? You have a problem with law and order?"

He shook his head. "Only when it gets stupid, and I'd just as soon we never get there."

"Fair enough."

Jess swung around in front of Jason, putting her feminine yet muscular arms around him. "You gonna stay home for a bit?"

He smiled. "Wild horses couldn't pull me away."

"Good," she said as she leaned in and up just a bit to kiss him. In that instant, the entire world seemed to vanish.

Simon clearing his throat, however, brought him right back to the here and now. "Sorry to interrupt, but there's still some work to be done."

Jason groaned as Jess glared at the other man. "You're interrupting my reunion because of work?"

Simon held both hands in front of him in mock surrender. "Just for a moment. After all, your husband did bring in some new people too."

"Make it fast. I've got plans for him tonight," she said with a mischievous grin and let her husband go.

He looked at his wife and smiled. "I'll make it quick."

She smiled back. "You'd better be talking about work and not later."

Chapter 2

Jason quickly recounted the Hernandez family's story, including the missing months. Simon agreed that it was suspicious, but without more to go on, there wasn't anything to worry about. A lot of people had things they didn't want to talk about. Just because it had been recent, rather than almost a decade ago, didn't mean it was something to be concerned about.

His home came into view as he rounded the bend in the rough, dusty road. While most of the houses in New Eden resembled the squares and rectangles people had lived in before the war, the Calvin homestead was a little different. Mounds resembling the bastard offspring of domes and cones overlapped one another, forming an unusual jumble that looked like something Jason remember from a science fiction movie. The top half was an odd mix of brush that made the house almost invisible from the tree line. Almost.

Opening the door, Jason took in the familiar sight. The main living space was round, like all of the rooms. The stark white limewashed walls contrasted with the deep wood of what little furniture adorned the room. A large, rough wooden table sat toward one side of the room, close to the primitive kitchen he and Jess built shortly after the house had been completed. A small rounded fireplace sat on the opposite side, the fire inside shooting light that ricocheted off the bright walls.

Jess sat on the worn leather couch the couple had scavenged from an abandoned home outside of Chattanooga a few years earlier, along with the leather recliner sitting at a right angle to it. Two battered end tables flanked the sofa. "All done?" she asked.

He nodded. "Yeah, just had to fill him in on the Hernandez family."

"They all good?"

He shrugged. "The committee will figure that out. At worst, they're a few extra hands for the fields. Who knows though."

"Be good to get some more skilled craftsmen."

He nodded as he made his way toward the recliner. "They're getting scarce."

"What do you expect. *People* were getting scarce for a while there."

"True. I'm just glad the expectations were wrong." Jason untied the leather thong holding his holster against his leg and unbuckled his gun belt, sitting it on the table next to him. He popped the foot part out and leaned back, stretching his arms out.

"Eight years of a nuke winter? I'd have rather they'd been more wrong." She shifted slightly toward her husband, curling her feet beneath her.

"Yeah, but since they thought we'd be looking at decades?"

"We think. No one knows how many weapons there were."

He nodded. "Maybe, but we know there were two in Georgia alone. I find it hard to believe it was that limited, you know?"

It was her turn to nod in agreement. "Wish we knew what else happened."

"Milton's counted up about twenty weapons hitting on our side."

"And how many did we launch?"

He shook his head. "No clue. He hasn't found anyone who watched any of the launches."

"He still looking?"

Jason shrugged. "With Milton? Who knows." He leaned up, the recliners back following his motion. "It's kind of hard to tell what Milton's going to care about from day to day, you know?"

"Yeah, so I've gathered. Still haven't met

the man myself."

"Hector wishes he could say the same," Jason said with a smile.

The rough wooden door swung open. Jason and Jess looked up to see their son enter the room. He was covered in head to toe with dirt, a usual thing for someone working in the fields.

"Hey, kiddo," Jason said.

Ricky looked at his father, a slight smile curling his lips. "Heard you'd made it back. Get 'em?"

Jason nodded. "Yep."

"Good. Maybe I can go out with you next time?"

"Not happening," Jess said.

"Sorry, kiddo. Your Mom has spoken."

Ricky groaned. "I'm seventeen now. I'm not some kid, you know."

Jason laughed, remembering telling his father the same thing at that age. Of course, he had to concede that Ricky had come of age in a much different world than he had. Ricky saw more dead bodies in the last decade than most morticians had seen in their entire pre-war careers. Still, to Jess, he was just a kid.

"What?" Ricky said defiantly.

"Just thinking about something else. I told my father the same thing is all," Jason said with a smile.

"Yeah, but that was different," he said, his voice inching louder.

"Maybe, but you're still living under this roof, and the rule in this town is eighteen or with parents permission, so you're stuck with it. Sorry."

Ricky rolled his eyes and stormed off to his room through a door to the left.

"Now that we've aggravated one of our kids, where's Allison?"

"Still at school. She should be back soon," Jess replied.

"You're kidding, right? It's almost supper time."

"She's learning more than reading and writing. It takes a bit longer, especially since they're trying to do so much of the traditional stuff too."

"Damn. Are they trying to graduate them at twelve?"

"Yeah, I get it. You're not a big fan of education in this day and age."

Jason slammed the footrest back into the recliner and leaned forward. "It's not that. I just don't think they're really doing right by the kids, that's all. They live in a different world, but they're leaving out some stuff they're going to need."

"No, they *were* leaving it out."

Jason was taken aback. "Were?"

She nodded. "Yep. I started teaching unarmed combat last week. Billy's agreed to teach firearm safety to the younger kids like Allison and then combat rifle and pistol shooting to the older kids in a couple of weeks." After her run-in with a warlord a decade ago, Jess had worked hard not to be a victim again. She learned how to fight from a former MMA champ that got stuck in the deep South after the war, far away from her home in California. Jason had taught her weapons. Jessica Calvin wasn't going to be a victim easily, that was for sure.

"What the hell happened?"

She shook her head. "Nothing really. I think some of what you said finally sunk in. With you not around though, they could make the decision without looking like they caved in to the sheriff."

He cocked his head to the side. "It's not like that. I was talking as a parent and you know it."

"Of course I do. They didn't. You've got to remember the lens they see you through. The sheriff. The hero. All that."

Jason groaned. "Don't start that hero shit again, alright? I just can't deal with that right

27

now."

"You don't have to deal with it. You've just got to know that it's what people think when they see you."

"I wasn't a hero. I was some kind of sociopath or something. That's not something to hold up and admire."

"And you're all better now?"

"Yes."

She smirked. "So who pulled the trigger on the Jones brothers?"

"That's different."

Her eyebrows rose as she said, "Oh? Do tell."

"They were cannibals. I'm sorry, but that makes them inhuman animals that need to be put down," he said defensively.

"They were people, Jason. Evil people, sure, but people. You killed them, and you don't feel any regret, do you?"

Jason leaned back in the chair, but said nothing. She was right, but he desperately wanted her not to be.

"And what about Baskin?" she asked

"What about him?"

"You were ready to blow him away, weren't you?"

He shrugged. "If he'd have been willing to do what he said he was, then yeah, I guess I would have."

Jess put her feet flat on the floor and leaned forward, resting her elbows on her knees, her arms tight against her body. "Babe, I love you, but you're lying to yourself if you keep trying to think you're the kind of guy you were before the war."

"I know I'm not. But I damn sure don't want to be that kind of guy I was right after it either."

"Because you're trying to live by standards that aren't really applicable anymore."

Jason sighed. "So not being a rabid animal isn't applicable?"

"It's not that," she said, standing and walking toward the kitchen space. "Damn it, Jason. I swear, sometimes it's like you're trying not to understand what I'm saying."

"You know that's not true," he said as he stood and followed her. "It's just...well, like it or not, I'm a product of that old world. It's against *that* world that I should be judged, not this one."

She turned to look at him. "Wrong. You spent years in that old world shooting matches, taking classes, all that stuff that got you ready for *this* world, not that one. You were more ready than most for what happened and you know it."

"So what do you want?"

"Just admit you're good at what you do. You're the kind of guy we need in this world. You're the kind of guy that can keep your family safe."

"And rescue damsels in distress from warlords?" he asked with a smile.

She smiled back. "Something like that," she said as she put her arms around him.

The door burst open, letting in a three and a half foot tall ball of fury. "DADDY!" she screamed.

Jess released her grip an instant before Jason dropped to his knees. "Come here, baby girl!"

Allison sprinted across the room, throwing herself into her father's arms. "Did you get the bad guys?"

He nodded. "We did, baby girl. We did."

"Good. Did Mommy tell you that she's going to teach us how to punch people?"

Jason smiled. "Yes she did. You know when to punch people and when not to, right?"

Allison nodded. "Mommy said we can punch people who are trying to hurt us or someone else, but that's it."

"Good girl. So...did you miss me?"

She smiled broadly and nodded.

"Good. How about you go get cleaned up

for supper and I'll help Mommy get it finished up?"

She nodded again and ran off toward her room.

** ** **

Jason milled around the market. Even this early in the season, fresh vegetables filled the stalls as barkers called out their wares, dozens of them blending into a chaotic cacophony that, when mixed with the smells of the vegetables, created a memorable impression that had burned itself into his memory.

"Mornin' Sheriff," an old lady at one of the stalls said. Jason tried to remember her name, but he wasn't completely sure he'd ever heard it before. New Eden grew more each week as outlying homesteads moved toward the safety of the town.

"Morning," he said with a smile.

He opened his mouth to ask about the green beans the woman had, but a familiar voice calling stopped him short. "Jason," he voice said.

Jason turned to see a mountain of a man, with skin like ebony, walking toward him. "What?" Jason barked.

"Don't even think about talking to me like

31

that, you puny piece of shit."

Jason's hand drifted toward his CZ-75B. "You sure you want to go down that road?"

The black man smiled. "Depends. Your mama's bed down that way?"

Jason smiled back. "No, but my Dad's is, and I bet that's more your speed."

The big man laughed. "About time you got your scrawny ass back here."

Joining him, Jason said, "Yeah, well, it took longer than I meant."

"At least you got the assholes."

"Yeah, but you know? Marshal Dillon didn't have to deal with people eating other people in Dodge City."

The other man shrugged. "Maybe it just didn't make it past the TV censors?"

Jason considered it for a moment, then shuddered. "Thanks, Billy. I didn't really need to think about that."

Billy chuckled. "You left it open, boss."

"All quiet while I was gone?"

"For the most part. Baskin started making some rumblings, but nothing we couldn't handle."

Jason nodded. "Man's got a right to make some rumblings, so long as it stays there."

"You comin' by the office?"

He considered it for a moment. In truth, he

hadn't. He was tired from three weeks in the saddle. On the other hand, it was kind of his job.

"Do I gotta?" Jason asked, a put on whiny tone coloring his words.

"Hey, I'm just the deputy," Billy said as he crossed his arms.

"Yeah, I'll be there in a minute."

"Good. Sully needs to talk to you about something."

Jason groaned. "Why do I doubt that it's about him finally qualifying with a handgun?"

"Probably because he still can't."

"Figures."

Billy laughed. "You're not going to turn him into a combat accountant, no matter how much you try."

"Great. Now I wish to hell I had a Larry Correia book to help the poor boy see the error of his ways," Jason said.

"You just want a new book to read."

"Fair enough."

The two men made their way down the dusty road, dandelions jutting up here and there, until they reached the New Eden jail. The two story building was one of the few brick buildings in town, built entirely of cinderblock then covered in stucco. The bottom floor served as an office for Jason and his people, while the upstairs was the actual jail. Iron bars covered all of the windows and were tightly bolted to the wall. For a post war town, it was an imposing structure.

Jason entered the main office. Four desks were placed facing each other in a square formation. The walls were relatively unadorned with the exception of a large map of the area. It had belonged to the forestry service before the war, so it lacked any of the newer settlements on it. Those had been marked on it with a black marker someone had scavenged.

Standing at one of the desks was Edward James Sullivan. To most everyone who knew him, he was just Sully. While most people in this day and age were thin, Sully was just scrawny. From what Jason could tell, the other man had never weighed more than he did right now unlike most folks these days. He was, however, very industrious in his field and had eagerly volunteered to maintain the inventories for the town. It was as close as he could get to actual accounting these days.

"How are you, sir?" Sully asked.

Jason nodded. "Fine. What did you need?"

"Yes, well...um...we've got a slight problem in the ammunition category, sir."

Jason raised an eyebrow. "What kind of problem?"

"It's 5.56, sir. We're down to about three thousand rounds of it."

He winced as he heard the number. "How much .308?"

"Not enough. We're down to about ten thousand of it."

Jason muttered under his breath. "Is there anything we're flush with?"

Sully shook his head. "We're better with 7.62x39 -about thirty thousand rounds- but if anything goes wrong, that might not be enough."

"That's wound down over the last six months. You know that," Billy volunteered, having entered behind Jason without a sound. Jason still wasn't sure how anyone that big could move so quietly.

"Any traders coming through?" Jason asked.

Sully shook his head. "Not with ammo. It's getting scarce. What we've got here, well, that might be all that's left in the whole valley. Either that, or people are holding on to it like Mama's pearls."

Jason considered for a moment. "Those are all military calibers, and I get that, but what about some of the civilian rounds?"

"Well, we've got plenty of .38 and .357. A good bit of 30-30, and some .44. That's about it," Sully said.

Jason nodded. "Keep checking. Someone's bound to have something. Grab whatever you can. We might be able to trade it later, alright?"

Sully nodded.

Noise erupted from outside the jail. All three men turned their head toward the door, still open to allow the occasional breeze to blow through the hot building. "What the hell?" Jason asked as he stepped out into the burning sun.

The jail was located on the central square. People were everywhere along the open green, clogging every road. Dark figures began to appear over the heads of the lollygaggers. People parted ways, like the Red Sea before Moses, allowing a column of horse mounted armed men step into the square.

He scanned the faces, trying to see if any were familiar. Each one was a stranger to him. *Either they're not local, or I really need to spend more time at home.*

In the lead was a large man, probably a foot taller than Jason, with a thick, dark beard and pale skin. He appeared to be wearing some kind of uniform, though it looked alien to Jason. "I'm looking for whoever is in charge in this settlement?" the man asked in a deep baritone.

"I guess I am," answered Simon, stepping out of the crowd. "Can I help you?"

"Yes, sir," the man said, then dismounted. "My name is Terry Conklin. My men and I have been trailing some escaped prisoners. We've got reason to believe they may have come through here. We'd appreciate any help you can give us."

Simon nodded. "Absolutely. Unfortunately, a lot of people come through here. I'm assuming you've got a description of them?"

Conklin nodded. "We do. Family. Man, his wife, and their kid. Hispanic. Man's named Mark Hernandez. His wife's name is Megan, their kid is Alexander."

Jason approached. "What did they do?"

The stranger turned to face him. "I'm sorry, friend. You are?"

Simon said, "That's Jason Calvin. He's the sheriff here."

Conklin smiled and offered his hand. "Ah, well then. Good to meet you."

Jason shook his hand. When they released their grips, Conklin continued, "They stole food. I'm sure you folks know how bad a crime that can be in these troubled times. It's not as bad now as it used to be, true, but it could still cost someone else their life."

"The kid's wanted too?" Jason asked.

Conklin nodded. "I'm afraid so. All three of them were caught with the food on their person.

Even admitted it in court."

Jason looked over at Simon. From the look on his face, it was clear Simon was thinking along similar lines.

"We'll see what we can find out for you," Simon offered. "In the mean time, feel free to set up camp outside of town. There's plenty of space. If you need to trade for supplies, again, help yourself. I'll let you know what I find out. Sound fair?"

Conklin's grin grew. "Absolutely, sir. I appreciate your help."

"In the mean time," Jason said, "mind if I ask where you folks come from? We're trying to get a feel for how the rest of the country's holding up."

Conklin nodded, his smile fading. "Somerton. A few days ride over the mountains."

Jason knew his surprise was written all over his face. "How are things that way?"

"Great. We're trying to rebuild as best we can. Extending protection all over. We'd offer it to you folks, but you're a bit outside of our range right now."

Jason nodded. He noticed that the other man didn't bother to ask if New Eden actually needed it or not though. Jason figured there was something telling in that.

Conklin remounted his horse and barked orders to his men. They turned and rode out of the square.

Simon walked over to Jason. "So, think we need to have a little chat with our guests?"

Jason nodded, his eyes never leaving Conklin's men until they were out of sight. "Yeah. Let's."

<u>Chapter 3</u>

The small man with jet black hair and dark skin called Ramirez looked over at his commander. "Think they know where they're at?" he asked.

Conklin nodded. "Absolutely. They know something at least, but everything says they're here. Let's try and keep an eye on the commander and the other guy if possible."

Ramirez nodded. "Yes, sir." He thought for a moment, then continued. "You don't think they'll hand them over, do you?"

Conklin looked at his lieutenant. "They might. It depends though. If they've still got them and know they're thieves, they might refuse simply because the scumbags stole from them too. I can respect that. Then again, they might think they're somehow better than us and won't hand them over no matter what."

"If that's the case?"

The larger man grinned wolfishly. "In that case, things get interesting."

Ramirez stifled a shiver. "I'll have Todd's team gather intel. Just in case."

The column had entered a large clearing. Conklin said nothing as he climbed off his horse. The small column that left the town met up with an additional two thousand men. Conklin was going to get those prisoners back, no matter what. "You do that, Ramirez. You do that."

Ramirez nodded and spurred his horse down the row of tents already erected, rows upon rows of them. Tents had been set up back to back, with a road running in front of each row of tents. Each placed precisely according to plan.

An attendant stepped forward to take the reins of Conklin's horse. The big man walked into his tent, dropping the flap to keep the world away. He was *going* to get these runners. He'd be damned if he'd let her get away from him. Not this time.

** ** **

Jason followed Simon, his mind in a thousand different directions, as they approached the church. Hardesty never actually used the rooms most folks called the parsonage. Instead, he typically used it to help out newcomer families. Singles could crash on someone's floor for a time, but families had special needs.

Mark and Megan sat at the dining table playing a card game. The couple looked up as the two men entered.

"We've got a bit of a problem," Simon said.

"Oh?" Mark asked.

"Yeah," Jason said. "Tell us about Somerton."

The couple's faces fell. "How...how did you hear about that?" Mark asked.

"Man named Terry Conklin just stopped by, looking for you. Said you were thieves," Simon said.

Mark cursed under his breath, then looked at the two men. "We're not. Nothing like that. I swear."

Jason pointed to a chair and gave a questioning look. Mark seemed to understand and nodded in reply. Sitting down, Jason looked at the couple. "Why don't you two tell us what the hell is going on? We've got armed men camped outside of town, which isn't fun for anyone, so why don't you fill us in."

"A few months back, we worked our way up through Alabama and into Tennessee. We were trying to get someplace cooler and this part of the country sounded like a better place than East Texas for that," Mark began.

Jason nodded. He couldn't say he could blame the guy.

"Well, we were running low on food and came across this house. The windows were busted, the door barely hanging on, all that stuff. It looked abandoned. Weeds grown up, the works. Well, we go in to see if there's anything there. We weren't holding out a lot of hope, but damned if there wasn't a couple of cans of soup."

Megan reached out and took her husband's hand. "The cans had a layer of dust on them. They'd been there a while." Jason nodded.

"So," Mark said, "we grabbed them. Later that day, we're eating them and these two guys come up on horseback. They're well fed and aren't acting aggressive or anything. Asked where we scored the food. They're not right up on us or anything, and they're pulling out their own food. I didn't see any harm, so I told them."

Jason raised an eyebrow and asked, "They were eating?"

Megan nodded. "Yes, sir. They just seemed curious, that's all."

He nodded for the couple to continue. "So, they ask us if we want to follow them back to town. Now, we're looking for somewhere to settle, and a town seems like the best place to do that obviously, so of course we said 'yeah'."

Megan picked up, "We get to town, and they lead us into this room. There's a guy sitting behind a desk. They tell him that we found a couple cans of food in this old house. I guess they knew the people who'd lived there, because they used a last name. Don't really remember what it was or anything, but I guess that doesn't really matter.

"Next thing we know, this guy asks if that's true. Well, we've scavenged before and it's always been understood that if no one's living in the house, whatever's left is fair game, so we say it is."

Again, Jason nodded.

"This guy announces we're guilty of theft and we're sentenced to lifetime indenture for our crimes. Not only that, but because Xander ate some of the food too, he's just as guilty and shares our sentences."

Simon leaned back in his chair. "Indenture?"

Mark nodded. "Yeah, that's what they call it. Your 'indenture' is then sold to someone and you have to do what they say. They can do whatever they want to you, and you can't do anything about it. Hell, they can kill you if they want, and there's nothing anyone can do about it."

"Sounds like slavery to me," Jason said, his brows furrowed.

Mark studied the table for a moment before finally nodding his agreement.

"So, you ran?" Simon asked.

Mark repeated the gesture.

"How long did you wait?"

Megan face grew defiant. Jason shifted his chair, ready to keep her from laying a hand on Simon. "We were fine until that sick fuck Conklin announced he'd bought me. Everyone knew what he did with the women he bought. He likes hurting people. I wasn't going to go through that."

Mark raised his head. "We had to run. If not, she'd have killed herself to avoid him. I don't think I could have blamed her."

Jason leaned forward. "Why didn't you tell us this when we found you?"

Mark shrugged. "I don't know. On one hand, it seemed so surreal, like something we saw in a movie or something. I mean, I thought slavery died with the Confederacy, you know? On the other, announcing we'd been convicted of stealing didn't seem like a smart introduction."

Man's got a point, Jason thought. The truth was, there wasn't any reason they would have. They didn't know where this town stood on slavery. While Mark may not have heard about slavery making a comeback after the war, Jason was intimately aware of how it worked. Jess had been taken for essentially the same purpose. He could still remember the feel of the knife in his hand as he put an end to that situation.

"Alright," Jason said. "You two lay low. When Xander gets back, he needs to lay low as well. We'll get you what you need."

"You're not...?" Mark stammered.

"Not my call, unfortunately," Jason said. "This is outside of my lane. The council will be dealing with this one. Simon's the chairman of it, but he's only one voice. However, I can tell you that I personally will do whatever I can."

"Same here," Simon said.

** ** **

It was late when Jason returned home. Word had gotten to Jess about what was going on, so the smell of stew filled the small house. Ricky, Allison, and Jess sat around the rough wooden table.

"Hungry?" Jess asked.

Jason nodded and forced a smile.

He pulled out a chair and sat down. Looking at his two children, he asked them about their day. Allison had gotten into a bit of a scuffle at school, which wasn't surprising. Older boys liked to try and push her around. Apparently, they figured because her father was sheriff, they'd get cool points for bullying her of all kids.

Unfortunately, the little bastards didn't realize that Allison was a fighter. Jess had started teaching her how to fight from the time she was old enough to throw a punch, and that was before she started teaching everyone at the school. Once as a damsel in distress in her life was more than enough, and she was determined her daughter wouldn't be one even once. At least Allison didn't break any bones. This time, anyway.

Ricky recounted his day in the fields, listening to guys who really didn't know anything, trying to be experts. The younger man simply nodded and did it the right way and moved on. Until the end of the day when he got the older man to describe how he wanted the beds prepared in front of Moonbeam, the hippy woman in charge of the gardening.

Jason laughed at the thought of the five foot two woman in overalls pulling a six foot six man down to eye level and educating him on the finer points of double dug beds.

Supper wrapped up and Allison went to bed, kissing Jason goodnight before turning in. He hated that he'd missed so much of her life.

Ricky announced he was meeting some friends at the pub someone had recently opened. Jason shook his head, imagining what his own father would have said if he'd said so openly that he was going out drinking. Of course, Ricky had grown up in a very different world.

Once they were alone, Jess asked, "So what's the deal?"

Jason filled his wife in on the details, including what the newcomers status was back in Somerton. With each sentence, her eyes seemed to widen more and more, as if she knew where this was going and couldn't believe it.

"So what's going to happen now?" she asked once the story was completed.

Jason shrugged. "No real clue. Simon will do what he can, and I promised them I would too, but it's up to the council."

She sighed.

"What?" he asked.

"The council," she answered.

Jason was confused. "What do you mean, 'the council'?"

"A bit of a change while you were out on that last hunt. Sam Morgan resigned. That put Cory Masters on."

Jason groaned, which elicited a nod from his wife. "Damn. A lot changes in a couple of weeks."

Cory Masters was unique, to say the least. Every name Jason had come up with for what type of person Masters was had been rejected. Jason saw no reason to insult dirtballs, shitbags, and weasels by associating them with Masters.

Unfortunately, Masters was a slick talker and could usually convince people of things.

"So Masters is likely to make things interesting?"

Jess nodded.

"Great."

"Look on the bright side," she said. "Maybe he'll decide to go along to get along for the time being."

Jason shot her an incredulous look. "Like he would miss a chance to screw stuff up just so he can say he's responsible for anything good that comes out of it?"

"Yeah, you're not that lucky," she said with a playful smile.

"Great. Just my luck," Jason said. "Is he stirring up anything yet?"

She nodded. "Yeah. He wants to have you recalled."

He rolled his eyes. "He's still pissed about that wheelbarrow, huh?"

"Well, he wanted it and you wouldn't sell it. Some people think the world owes them a living. Cory's one of them. What are you going to do?"

"I should have beaten him down when I had the chance."

She laughed. "And then he'd have had even more reason to try and stir up crap for you than he already does."

Jason cocked his head in agreement. Still, it would have been pretty satisfying to have at least done something to earn this kind of animosity.

"Think he'll be a problem?" Jason asked.

Jess shrugged. "Not sure. It depends on how many others on the council listen."

"He's only got to convince two of them."

She nodded. "And Evans seems to disagree with you on general principle, so she'll be easy."

Jason thought about the remaining three members. Simon was a no-go. He knew that for a fact. That left Mitchell and Reid.

"He'll get to Reid eventually. The guy is spineless."

She nodded. "So what'll happen then?"

He shrugged. "Damned if I know."

** ** **

The next morning, Jason entered his office. As usual, Billy was already at work. Hector was as well, sitting at one of the desks used by deputies in general. "Glad you made it," Billy said.

"There was a doubt?" Jason asked, thrown off by welcome.

"Had someone try and hit the Wayne homestead last night."

"How bad?"

"It wasn't. Jeff had some folks over for a card game, and they were all armed, so they handed the raiders their asses."

"Alright. I don't see the problem."

Billy held out his hand, a strip of yellow cloth hanging off from either side of his massive paw.

Jason took the armband. It was red with a yellow triangle stitched onto it, a symbol Jason had seen before. Swearing under his breath, he handed it to Hector.

"Brotherhood?"

Jason nodded. "Looks like."

"Son of a bitch. I thought we were done with those assholes."

"Not until we kill the last one, apparently."

"Who?" Sully said from behind Jason. He'd not heard the little man enter the room.

"Brotherhood of the Disgraced Pyramid. They tell people they're agents of the Illuminati, former Freemasons who brought about the war and now seek dominion over all mankind." Jason said.

Hector nodded. "The problem is, it's all a bunch of horseshit."

"How can you be sure?" Sully asked.

Jason rolled up his sleeve, revealing a tattoo, the compasses and square of a master Freemason. "I'm sure because I am a

51

Freemason. I've been slogging it out with everyone else since the war. Trust me, if there was some easy path to the good life, I'd have taken it."

"He's right. They're just raiders hiding behind conspiracy theories, using them to scare the hell out of the gullible," Hector added.

"You find anything else?" Jason asked, turning his attention back to Billy.

The big man shook his head. "Besides their gear? Nothing."

"Well that's a complication we didn't need."

"The Hernandez family?" Billy asked.

Jason nodded. He trusted the three men in this room with his life, so he filled them in on everything he and Simon learned the previous evening.

"You've got to be shitting me," Hector said, his mouth hanging open.

Shaking his head, Jason said, "I wish. Of course, they might have also escaped from a regular jail and are lying. We've got to figure out if they're telling the truth."

"Yeah, um…you realize that calls for 'subtle', right?" Bill said.

"Hey! I can do 'subtle'."

Billy and Hector looked at one another for a moment before bursting into laughter. Sully decided to exhibit infinite wisdom and opted to leave the room before he joined the other two.

"Yeah, laugh it up." Jason said, clearly not enjoying being the target of their mirth. "Of course, there's always another option."

Hector stopped laughing.

"Don't make me go. That's all I ask. I swear, I'm going to deck that stoner the next time he asks if I'm legal or not."

"I guess he can't imagine how a Hector Martinez could possibly be an American. For that matter, I guess he can't imagine that the United States doesn't exactly exist anymore," Jason said, his enjoyment growing at his second-in-command's discomfort.

"Just leave me behind. That's all I ask." The big man's discomfort had him shifting in his seat.

Jason laughed. "Don't worry. We're going to head that way. I'll deal with Milton while you can be safely busy doing something else."

Hector looked up toward the blue sky and made the sign of the cross on his chest. "Thank you, Lord. Thank you."

Billy was still laughing, now at his friend's near miss.

"You can go instead," Jason said to Billy with a huge grin.

The big black man stopped laughing as Hector turned and started.

"That's not funny, Jason. Not funny at all."

"Sure it is. For me it's freaking hysterical," he said, relishing the other man's discomfort.

<u>Chapter 4</u>

Simon was waiting at his dining table when Jason walked through the door. Jess sat across from him, each with a cup of tea in front of them. Simon looked serious. "Uh, hi," Jason stammered out. After a long day, he wasn't exactly expecting the other man.

"Heard about the attack on the Wayne homestead. Any luck?" Simon asked.

Jason shook his head. "Nope. Jeff and his buddies had all the luck last night. Found out who they were though."

"Well, that sounds like a bit of luck then," Jess offered.

"Not really. Looks like the Brotherhood are back."

Simon sighed. "Just what we need."

Jason pulled out a chair and sat down next to Jess. "Tell me about it."

"Well, I'm sorry to pile on more bad news, but the council's having a meeting tomorrow night," Simon said.

"I don't suppose it's about upping how much we're paid?" Jason asked.

"You wish," Simon said, smiling slightly at

the old joke. "It's about the Hernandez family."

Jason sighed and turned his gaze upward. "Not what I needed."

Simon nodded. "Yeah, I know. Masters has been talking a lot of crap and it's got to be dealt with."

"Let me guess. Masters, Evans and Reid."

Simon nodded.

Jess looked at her husband knowingly.

"They want to hand them over."

Simon nodded again.

"Great. This town is governed by you and some morons."

The chairman shrugged. "Nah. Mitchell's alright."

"But no argument on the other three?"

He shook his head. "None."

"Good. The last thing I needed to hear was that they were the real brain trust running this town."

"The good news is that they want your input. You'll be at the meeting, right?"

Jason nodded.

"Great. In that case-"

"In that case," Jess interrupted, "someone's going to have to keep Jason calm." The look she gave Jason made it clear that he wasn't to deny needing someone for such a purpose. He was about to protest anyway, but the truth was that she was right. Dealing with idiots was never a pleasant thing.

Chapter 5

The next morning, Jason walked to his office. The council meeting was later tonight, and he wasn't looking forward to it. Sitting outside was Hector. The deputy was trying to look relaxed, and might have fooled people who didn't know him as well as Jason did.

"What's up?"

Hector looked back at him. He didn't twitch a muscle, but his body loosed up from relief. "Someone inside to see you. Billy wanted me to give you heads up."

"Why?"

The deputy shrugged. "No clue. He caught me before I got through the door."

Jason nodded as he opened the door. Inside, he saw his friend sitting with an unknown man in the same uniform as Conklin's troops. Both men stood as Jason strode up to the Billy's desk.

"Billy," Jason said before turning his attention to the other man.

"Boss, this is Al Holliman. He says he's with the Somerton Resistance Movement."

Jason shot his friend a surprised look. Billy

simply nodded in acknowledgement.

Holliman pretended not to notice, but instead held out his hand. "Mr. Calvin."

Jason shook the hand. "Jason, please."

The other man nodded.

"So, I assume you wanted to speak with me about something?"

Holliman nodded. "Yes, sir. Unfortunately, I need to tell you that your home is being watched, as is the Chairman's. I figured it made more sense to come here and request a meeting. I figure you were followed, but they'll leave when you do as well."

"Understood. I'm assuming that's not why you wanted to speak to me, right?" Jason said as he sat down.

"No, sir. It's about the Hernandez family."

Jason raised an eyebrow.

Holliman took a deep breath before continuing. "By the laws of the Republic of Somerton, they're guilty of theft, but you need to know that it's only in the most ridiculous way possible."

The phrasing of that surprised Jason a bit. *Republic of Somerton?* Instead of letting the words slip past his lips, he said, "Do tell.".

"After the war, we had it as bad as I suspect the rest of Tennessee had it. The winter wasn't pleasant and food got scarce. Conklin, saying he was speaking for the mayor, declared all food not currently in private hands belonged to the town. Then he kept expanding the town's borders, usually without telling the folks who lived there until afterward."

"Really?"

Holliman nodded. "Unfortunately. Then, a couple of years ago, he decided that the town of Somerton was just too damn big to be a town, so he changed it to the Republic of Somerton."

"And the slavery thing?"

Holliman nodded. "Conklin's idea to keep people from leaving the area."

"Huh?" Billy said. "Why would he care?"

"Because tyrants need subjects, right? Jason asked.

The Somerton trooper nodded. "Exactly. He says he's doing this for the mayor - who he now calls the governor - but no one's seen the 'governor' in over eight years. We're not even sure he's alive."

"So you figure Conklin either knocks the governor off, or takes advantage of him dying of natural causes and seizes power."

Holliman nodded. "That's pretty much it."

"And the slaves?"

"When he started with the indenture, it was supposed to be a temporary thing. Someone would get sentenced to two years indenture, and then someone bought the bond and had labor for a couple of years. Then the sentences became more and more draconian until before long, all the sentences were for life."

"So what do you want from us?" Jason asked.

"Don't send the Hernandez family back. Conklin figures they came through here, but he doesn't know if they're still here or not. If they are, tell him they're not. For their sake."

"I've heard Conklin is a little rough with the women," Jason said.

"You've heard wrong," Holliman said. As Jason began to think of what that might mean, Holliman continued, "He's a sadistic bastard that likes to hurt people. Women in particular. I know what you meant, but I've seen the aftermath of what he does to these women. I know you were being fascias, but it's just too bad to even do that. Not for me anyways."

"Alright, so he's a mean son of a bitch. All you want is for us to not help Conklin out? I mean, if this guy's so bad, why not ask us to take him out for you?"

Holliman gave a pained grin. "Because he outnumbers you four to one, at least."

"You guys only had a few dozen follow him into the square?"

"Yeah, but that was just a small honor

guard. He had over two thousand waiting for him."

"For a single family?"

"I'm not sure what the deal is. I mean, Megan Hernandez is attractive enough, but the whole damn state could be falling apart right now. I still haven't figure out what his deal is on this one," Holliman confided.

"I'm sure you'll understand if we don't take your word for all of this?"

He nodded. "I wouldn't believe me, so I understand it completely. Hell, I've seen it all first hand, and I'm not sure *I* believe me."

Jason looked at Billy. The big man nodded his understanding.

Holliman said, "If it's alright with you, I'd like to wait a little while here after you leave. I'd rather your watcher didn't see me."

"Of course. Billy, in a little while, let him out the back," Jason said as he stood and left the room, Billy right beside him.

"He gave us the location of their campsite when he got here. I've already got Jimmy Peterson taking a look," Billy said as soon as they were out of earshot.

Jimmy Peterson was the most skilled hunter in New Eden. While most people had starved, he'd still managed to find game through the long winter and kept his family feed. If he didn't want to be seen, he wouldn't be.

"Let me know in the morning if he finds anything," Jason said. He knew they would. Holliman might not be completely above board on everything, though Jason was inclined to buy his story, but he saw zero reason for Holliman to lie about numbers that could be so easily checked.

Billy nodded.

** ** **

Jess knocked on the door to the parsonage, a canvas bag weighing down the hand opening the door. "Hello?" she called out.

Megan Hernandez peeked around the corner, drying a dish. "Hi!" she said cheerfully.

"I'm Jessica Calvin. I believe you've met my husband?" She stepped toward the other woman with her hand extended.

Quickly drying the dish, Megan sat it down and took the other woman's hand. "Oh! Mrs. Calvin? You're Jason's wife?"

"That's me. Please, call me Jess," She said with a smile. "I brought you guys some stuff. You've been kind of cooped up here for a little while and figured you could use it." She held out the bag.

Megan took it and sat it down on the small

kitchen table. Her eyes widened as she looked inside, cutting them back toward Jess. "We can't take this. I appreciate it, but..." She held up a ripe tomato larger than her fist.

"Sure you can. A lot of us kicked in what we could. No one who couldn't afford to give it up though," Jess said with a smile. She'd always been told she had a million dollar smile, and figured this might be a good time to use it.

"You sure?"

Jess nodded. "Absolutely. A few things from a lot of people adds up pretty quickly, you know?"

Megan nodded her understanding.

She continued. "There *is* another reason I came by."

"Oh?" Megan asked.

Jess hated this part. She hated that Jason hadn't done it already, but she figured he was a little preoccupied with everything going on, hence why she was here. "There's a meeting of our governing council tonight."

"Oooookay?" she said, her confusion obvious to Jess.

"They're going to be talking about you three. What to do about you guys, to be specific."

Megan pulled out a chair and sat, dropping her head into her hands.

Jess continued, "For what it's worth, Jason's going to fight for you three. If he can't win the council over, well...I know my husband. If he says he has no intention of handing you over, then you're probably not going to be handed over if he can do anything at all to prevent it."

She looked up. "He's not going to break the law though, right?"

Jess shrugged. "Knowing my husband? I don't put anything out of the realm of possibility."

"He's a good man," Megan said with a sorrowful smile.

"He is, but he's something more than that. He's a righteous man. He's got a sense of right and wrong, and he kind of sticks by that, regardless. He doesn't *realize* that, but that's who he is."

"You seem to know your husband better than he does."

"What wife doesn't?" Jess said with her own smile.

Megan laughed. "True."

"I'll keep you in the loop, so don't worry about that. I know how much it sucks being blindsided, so I'll do what I can to make sure that doesn't happen."

Megan's laugh subsided, but she smiled painfully.

"I've got to run. I'll come back tomorrow and let you know about what happens at the meeting, alright?"

Megan nodded. "Thank you."

Jess put her hand on the other woman's shoulder, squeezing gently and then leaving the church.

The air outside was stifling. After years of perpetual winter, she was beginning to sympathize with northerners who had moved south. She'd kind of made fun of them back before the war for their inability to deal with the southern heat, which was generally returned come winter time. Now, the heat was impacting her.

She muttered apologies for all the harassment she'd offered as she wiped the already forming sweat from her brow.

Outside of the church, a busy roadway bustled with people pushing carts to and from the small market in the town square just a few dozen yards away. Reverting to old habits, Jess looked both ways before crossing the busy trail. Left, then right, then left again.

Her brain processed the view to the right a bit slow. She had been focused on traffic, what else she'd seen hadn't really registered immediately. Without meaning to, her head shot back toward the right.

John Baskin stood off to the side of the road. Still dressed in his non-matching black clothing, he was talking to two men, though Jess used the term as loosely as possible. *Oh, this isn't good.*

The three looked at her, hatred etched on their face. They made no move toward her, so she opted to simply cross the road and look for her husband.

** ** **

For the third time since he'd been home, he stood outside Mrs. Marshall's house and tried to explain reality to the old lady. "I understand that the chickens can get kind of loud, but Horace's had that coop there since before you came to New Eden. I'm not going to tell him to move it. I'm sorry, but he's got the right to do what he wants on his property."

"But they wake me up too early in the morning," she argued.

"I'm sorry about that, but they're chickens. It's something they do. You knew that when you had your house built here."

"I did not!" she protested. "He built that coop just last week."

Jason fought the urge to roll his eyes. "No, ma'am, he didn't. It's been there a long time."

"I'm going to go to the magistrate," she said, a crooked finger point up at his face.

He smiled. "If that's what you think you need to do, go right ahead. That's certainly your right."

"I'll take *you* before the magistrate, too!"

He forced his smile wider. "That's also your right."

Jason turned and began walking away when he caught sight of Jess moving toward him. He shifted his direction to meet her. He face betrayed her concern.

"Hey, babe. What's up?"

She recounted the sight from outside the church. "It might not mean anything, but I don't see John Baskin trying to tell the Elias brothers to repent of their evil ways. He hasn't got the balls for it."

Jason nodded. The Elias brothers were trouble, and they were allegedly connected trouble. Rumor had it that they'd run the crime in a small town in northern Alabama before the war and used their cutthroat methods to survive. Jason never gave all that much credence since people like that tended to go raider instead of settling down in small communities. Instead, Jason pegged them as petty crooks who saw an opportunity in New Eden that didn't exist in a lot of places.

"Thanks for letting me know," he said.

"You got a plan?"

Jason shook his head. "It's not illegal to talk to people. Not much I can do except keep an eye out."

"You don't think he's still pissed about you bringing Katie back, do you?"

He smiled. "Oh, he's still pissed. Baskin's still pissed about a wedgie he got back in high school. That man can hold onto a grudge until it dies of old age."

"Maybe he wants the brothers to do something?"

Jason shrugged. "Maybe. Like I said, I'll keep an eye out, so no need to worry," he said with a smile.

She nodded.

He smiled at her, the freckles across her nose always making her look more youthful than him, regardless of their similarities in age. *Besides, I'm already stressing enough shit with the council meeting tonight.*

** ** **

Jason hated politics. His philosophy had always been "to each their own". Unfortunately, that seemed far too complicated for most politicians, which were something else he generally didn't like. Simon may have technically been a politician, but he was the exception in Jason's mind. The rest were in there for power and nothing more.

The room was unusually empty. Normally, when the council met, at least half of the seats were filled. Most didn't care about the day to day operations of the council so long as there was food available, but a few liked to keep up on what was happening. Without TV and newspapers to tell them, they figured they'd best sit in and find out.

A long table stretched across the front of the room. Jason wasn't sure, but the table looked like it was made out of cherry that had been polished to a shine. The work itself was impressive since Jason remembered when it had been commissioned. The man who made it died a short time later, but he truly had been a master of using hand tools to craft wood. It was a shame his skills were gone.

Behind the table, the council members sat. Simon, as chairman, was in the center. Mildred Evans and John Mitchell sat to Simon's left. To his right, Cory Masters occupied a seat, followed by Zack Reid to Master's. The council secretary sat at the end of the table, a stack of paper in front of her.

Simon looked around for a moment before

speaking. "I'm going to call this meeting to order. As we all know, the matter for discussion is the disposition of the Hernandez family. They were allegedly convicted of theft under laws outside of our jurisdiction. Sheriff Jason Calvin has looked into the matter, as I understand. Is that correct?"

Jason nodded. "It is, Mr. Chairman."

"Your findings?"

Jason recounted what he had learned, keeping Holliman's identity secret. While he trusted Simon, he wasn't so sure about some of the other councilors.

When he finished, Masters spoke. "Mr. Chairman, may I ask Sheriff Calvin some questions?"

Simon nodded, but he didn't like it. Anyone looking at the man's face could see it.

"Sheriff Calvin, you say this information came to you via a member of Mr. Conklin's outfit?"

"Yes, Councilor."

"And you consider this information credible?"

"I do."

"And just what makes you think that?"

"Because it corroborated what the Hernandez family told myself and Chairman Redfeather."

"And it's not possible that this was arranged before hand by the Hernandez family?"

Jason didn't have a poker face. He knew it. It's part of why he didn't play poker for money. Everyone in the room, in that particular moment, also knew he had no poker face. They also knew exactly what flavor of idiot he figured Cory Masters was. Everyone, apparently, except Cory Masters.

"Answer the question, please, Sheriff."

Jason took a deep breath, desperate to hold onto what self control he had left. "Councilor, when we recovered the Hernandez family, they were about to be carved into steaks by the Jones Brothers. They have been surrounded by people of New Eden since that moment. At no point has there been any reports of any stranger entering the church, where they've been since arriving in town.

"Frankly, I find the suggestion not only unlikely, but ridiculous. For it to have happened, the Hernandez family would have had to have planned on having a partner travel some distance away but still able to make contact from time to time. That same partner would have had to be willing to leave their companions to the tender mercies of cannibals, while still being willing to step up to keep them from being taken back to Somerton."

"I'm sorry, Sheriff, but I don't appreciate your tone," Master said, drawing himself up to look superior. "I am an elected member of this council."

"That's enough," Simon interjected. "Your question was asked, and it was answered. As for Sheriff Calvin's assessment of the likelihood of your theory, I'm afraid I have to agree."

With that, the council erupted in each person speaking at one time, the various sounds merging into a cacophony of chaos. Simon began slamming his gavel onto the piece of wood on the table, the loud crash echoing over the disquiet voices.

A moment after the gavel began its banging, the voices settled down. Simon twisted his head, as if trying to ring out the experience out of his mind. "Now, councilors, I will remind you that we cannot discuss anything with any meaning if we all speak at once."

Masters slapped the table and he pushed himself up. Looking down on Simon, he said, "You and your comments were out of line."

"No they weren't." All eyes shifted to the other end of the table, toward John Mitchell. "Truth is, you're looking for a reason to hand this family over to this Conklin fella. Before tonight, I might have agreed with ya. Ain't none of our business what they done or where they done it, but on the same token, it ain't our fight.

"If they done wrong, they should pay. Here's the thing about being old though, and you, Mr. Masters, might want to listen in case you ever make it there. Folks 'll talk to ya when they won't talk to most others."

The old man grinned slyly. Jason really didn't know John Mitchell, but something said he wasn't done talking.

"Well?" Masters said, his voice dripping with sarcasm. "Out with it. Just what did they tell you?"

"The same damn thing Jason's been tellin' ya. What are you? Stupid?" Mitchell asked furiously.

The laughter broke from Jason before he'd realized it. Struggling, he stifled further laughing at the councilor's expense. Simon maintained better self control, but not by much, his face straining from the effort.

Masters was beet red. His eyes darted to his two allies, neither of whom bothered to return his gaze.

"Mr. Chairman? If I may?" Jason said, hoping the act of speaking would refocus him on the task at hand.

Simon nodded.

"Councilors, we have three sources giving remarkably similar accounts. That doesn't happen by accident. Hell, I was a reporter before the war. I would interview multiple eye-witnesses to an event and often not get the same story from any two of them not necessarily the same. The fact that we're getting stories so similar tells you there's truth to them.

"Now, I can't tell you what to do, but I can tell you that there is ample reason to believe that Megan Hernandez is in grave danger if returned to Somerton. There is also ample reason to believe that they are candidates for asylum if nothing else. I simply ask that you think on this for a few days before you turn this family over to Conklin."

Heads nodded around the table, including Evans and Reid surprisingly.

"A hell of an idea," John Mitchell barked. Jason was beginning to regret not getting to know the councilor better.

It was agreed, even Masters grudgingly conceding to Mitchell's wisdom. The next several minutes consisted of some more mundane matters that didn't seem to really impact anything, including the agenda for their next public meeting. None of it really mattered to Jason, so he zoned out and thought about a conversation with Billy earlier.

Holliman had been right. Big shock. Thousands of troops camped right outside New

Eden. The town's militia might not be bad, but they only had a few hundred men they could mobilize in town at any given time. At most, he had another two hundred out on various patrols or hunting expeditions. They couldn't win a straight up fight. He had some serious planning to do.

The shuffling of chairs pulled Jason's thoughts back to the here and now. The meeting was breaking up, so he stood and waited for Simon. John Mitchell nodded to him, which Jason gladly returned. The old man was a tough old bastard apparently, and Lord knows the town needed that these days.

The other councilors passed him by. Only Masters looked at him, the newest member firing daggers at Jason with his eyes. Jason simply smiled and nodded politely.

"You just love antagonizing people, don't you?" Simon asked as he walked up.

Jason shrugged. "Love it? Not sure. But it does come natural."

The chairman laughed. "At least it was Masters. You're lucky that Mitchell stepped in when he did."

He nodded. "Yeah, I am. It was almost too convenient."

Simon leaned in and whispered, "That's because he's full of shit."

Jason looked at the other man, puzzled.

"Mitchell didn't talk to a damn soul. He could see you were telling the truth, so he said something that would shut Masters up."

"That dirty, old bastard," Jason muttered as he grinned in admiration.

Simon shrugged. "I told you he was alright."

Smiling, Jason said, "He is at that."

"So what's next?"

"Got to go see Milton."

"Really?"

Jason nodded. "Not really any way around it. He's the only one wired in anymore."

Simon chuckled. "That's one way to put it."

Holding his hands out, palms up, Jason asked, "What? Why does everyone think he's that bad?"

Chapter 6

Conklin sat on the folding chair. It was a lovely design that looked like a regular chair but could collapse for easy travel. The craftsman who made it swore the design dated back to the American Revolution. Conklin didn't give a damn. He just liked having nice things around. Not surprising for a man who'd grown up with nothing.

The trooper entered the tent and saluted. Conklin wasn't about to get up for a mere private. Instead, he nodded, which told the trooper he had permission to drop the salute. His men were disciplined. A lot more so than the rabble Calvin commanded. His "troops" were just militia.

"Report," Conklin barked.

"Sir," the trooper said as he held out the note in his hand. The paper had been folded in three and sealed with wax. It was an old technique, but it worked well enough to see if a note had been read without permission.

Conklin nodded again. The trooper threw up a quick salute, then spun and exited the tent.

Taking a knife from his belt sheath, he

pried the seal open to read the contents. As his eyes drank in the words, the corners of his mouth curled up into a smile.

So close now. Oh so close.

** ** **

Milton Thompson was probably the last of the Dot Com millionaires. After he had cashed out of Silicon Valley, he'd packed up his wife and moved to the mountains of Tennessee. Despite the piles of money he'd made with technology, he'd felt that man was losing touch with what had made mankind thrive. That, and he figured it would be easier to pay the mountain cops to look the other way when it came to what he called his "special garden".

The house wasn't particularly large, but was a decent size ranch style house. Dark brown with trim running vertically on the house every couple of feet, kept it from looking like the millions of other ranch houses. Behind the house was a Quonset style greenhouse about the size of a football field, which was the most unique thing about the house.

"Why did I have to come," Hector asked, his voice reminding Jason more of Ricky before the war than an experienced fighter.

"I needed someone to watch my back on

the trip and Billy's wife got sick," Jason said. In reality, the three day trip was mostly through New Eden territory, and therefore relatively safe. Unfortunately, relatively safe didn't mean a whole lot in the grand scheme of things. Luckily, it had been uneventful.

"Yeah, that's why he was laughing at me after he told you," he muttered.

"That's true, but seniority has its perks." Jason was enjoying his deputy's discomfort as he pulled up short on the horses outside the front door. Jason knew from experience that Milton knew they were there already. Walking up to the door and knocking, Jason pondered what kind of mood the strange man would be in.

Milton swung the door open, his eyes wild. Jason looked at the older man but barely recognized him. While Milton was normally fairly clean cut, he now sported a scraggly beard, though fairly short. Jason shot a look at Hector in askance. Hector shrugged.

"Milton?" Jason asked, unsure of what the answer would be.

The scruffy man's eyes widened, a smile cracking through the bird's nest of a beard. "Jason! So good to see you, my boy!"

Jason smiled. "Good to see you too. You remember Hector?" he asked.

Milton nodded. "Yes, oh yes, I remember. I

remember him well. Very well indeed. I hope he has his green card on him, oh indeed I do."

Hector sighed.

"Please," Milton continued, "come on in, boys, come on in. You don't want to be outside too long. *They'll* see you, oh yes they will. They'll see, and they'll know."

Jason knew Milton was weird. Hell, *Milton* knew that Milton was weird. It wasn't breaking news, but something wasn't quite right. Regardless, he and Hector entered the house after tying off their horses to the front porch railing.

The interior of the house was only spectacular in that it hadn't changed much since the war; sheetrock walls painted warm colors faded slightly over the years, photographs of now long dead friends and family. It looked almost like any other house before the war would have. More than a decade later, however, it was a time capsule of a nearly forgotten era.

"Sit, sit, go ahead and sit. We can talk then, oh yes, we can talk," Milton said, pointing to the slightly worn couch. Hector looked at Jason, who just nodded his head. Their host acted more bizarrely than usual.

Milton seemed oblivious to their concern as he looked over his shoulder. Jason followed the other man's eyes with his own. Two young women, probably in their early twenties, if that, walked into the room. Both were stunning, one blonde and the other a redhead, with all the right curves. Unlike a lot of women post-war, they clearly hadn't gone without food, which made sure they had those curves. "Ah, ladies, meet my friends, oh yes, please do meet my friends. This is Jason, Jason Calvin, and that is Hector. I forget Hector's last name, but his first is Hector."

"Martinez", Hector volunteered.

"Oh, that's right. Hector, Hector Martinez, that's his name." He turned his attention to the two young ladies and put his arm around both. "This is Debbie and Marti. They're new, oh yes, they're oh so new. They're here now, hopefully be here awhile, but who knows how the world will shake out in the grand scheme of things?"

Jason leaned forward, sitting just on the edge of the couch with his forearms resting on his knees. "Milton? What happened to Connie?" Connie was Milton's wife. She was usually the one who kept Milton settled down. Truth was, she handled most any interaction that happened outside of the house, and most inside as well.

"Oh, Connie? Connie went buh-bye," he said, his hand waving at nothing. "She went buh-bye, oh yes, she did. Will she come home? Maybe, maybe not. But I've got Debbie and

Marti here with me now, oh yes, Debbie and Marti are here with me now."

The two women watched Jason and Hector, seeming more predator than ally. "Ladies," Jason said, nodding to the two women. Both smiled back but said nothing.

"So, my friends, my very good friends, what can I do for you? Oh yes, what can I do for you today?" Milton asked.

"I'm curious what you're hearing out of the Somerton area? Anything?"

"Somerton? Not much, oh no, no much at all. Why worry about Somerton anyways? It's all the way over in Somerton, after all."

Jason had a very bad feeling. Milton could be odd, to say the least, but he was raving like a mad man. This wasn't even close to normal. Not even for Milton.

"Are you alright?" Jason asked.

"Oh, I'm fine, oh so fine. We've just got to keep away from them, oh they are out there, waiting and watching. They started the whole war, you know. It was all them, all them. The Freemasons, you know, they did it all!"

Jason rolled up his sleeve, revealing the tattoo. "Milton, it's not the Freemasons. See?" he asked pointing to the tattoo. "I am one. We didn't do it, alright?"

Milton's eyes widened in surprise. "So you

know! You know all about it. No wonder you made it, no wonder you survived. They made sure you made it, didn't they?"

Jason shook his head. "No, they didn't. I got lucky. Just like a lot of people." Hector groaned softly enough that only Jason could hear it.

"Oh? They didn't warn you?"

Jason shook his head. "No. No one warned me."

"They screwed you over? That's awful! But don't you worry, my boy, because we're in this together, oh yes we are. All in this together..." The older man trailed off, a bit of the wildness drained from his eyes. His two companions kept their focus on the two visitors.

"So, you've got nothing on Somerton?" Jason asked, already knowing the answer.

"Nope. Not a thing, nothing at all, but that's all the way over in Somerton, so no need to fret none on that count, don't you know?"

"Alright. Thanks, Milton. I appreciate your time. I guess Hector and I need to be running. Got a few other stops to make on the way home."

Milton nodded. "Okay, okay, my boy, you run on if you must, oh if you must. You'll come back some other time in the oh so near future?"

"Of course we will," Jason said with a

smile.

Milton smiled as the two lawmen walked through the door.

After a few quick goodbyes, the door closed. The two men mounted their horses and began the trip back toward New Eden.

"That guy gets more fucked up every time I see him," Hector said after half an hour.

"Maybe when you see him, but that was different, even for him."

"How so?"

"He and his wife, Connie? They've been absolutely nuts for one another for ages. Ever since I met them, it's been like Gomez and Morticia Adams. Weird, but also kind of cute, you know? But now she just up and left? Really?"

"Maybe the weird was getting to her?"

Jason shook his head. "No, I don't think so. There's something else going on. If nothing else, the guy is loaded down with food and he does most of the work. That greenhouse? He works it, he cooks the food, he cans it, the works."

"That *is* weird. Hell, I could put up with a lot of crazy if for the easy life these days."

"Exactly. Most would. Why in the hell would she leave?"

The big man shrugged. "No clue, boss."

"Me neither."

** ** **

The horses were exhausted as they whipped through the woods at speeds no sane person would chance during a trip filled with tree limbs, holes, and any number of other things. The Jason, Hector, and the two militiamen who had met up with them on the trip back were far from sane at this moment.

All the two men had said was that there was some kind of an attack. They weren't sure who was responsible. Jason didn't care just now. The two messengers didn't know if either his or Hector's family were hurt or not. They needed speed to find out.

Small branches whipped against Jason's face, stinging his cheeks as the branch tips dug into his skin. He ignored it. His mind filled with visions of his family massacred, his home burned to the ground, and the town in complete disarray.

The smell of smoke invaded his nostrils, fueling his imagination as they got close. Each heartbeat brought new terrors from deep in his psyche.

As the town came into view, some of those visions seem all too real. Several homes had been torched, leaving nothing but smoldering ruins. Slaughtered livestock littered the ground.

They slowed. People ran with little heed for anything else, their tasks occupying every corner of their minds.

The four riders guided their horses through the chaos. Jason didn't give a damn about the town right then. Hector peeled off as they got close to his home. Jason barely noticed, his eyes scanning the casualties, lined up near the church in the town square, for his family. He saw none of them. It was just the wounded. His loved ones' absence did nothing to alleviate his anxiety.

The three remaining riders turned the corner, bringing Jason's house into view. For the first time in two days, he felt himself relax just a bit. The house looked unscathed.

When they got outside the house, he dropped from his mount and ran for the door, throwing it open. "Jess?"

His wife sat on a chair turned backwards, her legs straddling the seatback. Ricky stood beside her, Jason's Mossberg 500 shotgun in his hand. Both turned their heads toward him.

In another chair, sitting in the middle of the room, was a man in a black Somerton uniform. His arms tied behind him, his mouth gagged, he'd been beaten pretty badly in the recent past.

"Welcome home, dear. I've got a present

for you," Jess said, her voice seductive but her eyes holding a glint of violence.

Jason stood in the doorway, stunned. "What the…?"

She smiled. "This asshole figured that a woman would be easy prey."

"Talk about your backfires, huh?"

Jason turned to the two militiamen beside him. "Let Billy know I'm here and that there's a prisoner. Can you let him know I need him when he gets a chance?"

The two men nodded, then left.

He turned his attention back to the man tied to a chair. "So, what did this 'gentleman' have in mind?"

Jess looked the man in the eye. "Well, Rusty here was just about to tell me all about that."

The man turned away, unable to meet her eye to eye.

"Answer her," Jason growled, his tone one he thought he'd lost over the last decade.

"Conklin…he told us to scare folks…smack them around…and…um…" Rusty stammered.

"And have your way with the women? Is that it?" Jason finished for the black shirted man.

He looked away before nodding.

"And your dumb ass picked Jess, huh?

Again, he nodded.

Jason shook his head and laughed.

The distinctive crack of gunfire came from outside. Jason's head jerked toward the still open door.

Ricky was already moving toward the door, shotgun at the ready. "Bastards keep coming back. Four times now."

Jason bolted for the door. He'd left his AK strapped to his horse. More gunfire echoed through the valley as four men in black uniforms - he'd started thinking of them as blackshirts - burst through the tree line about forty yards away. There was no way he'd get the rifle unstrapped in time, so he pulled his pistol. The CZ-75B was a personal favorite of his, but it hadn't left the holster for some time.

The four men sprinted toward the Calvin's, screaming like demons. Ricky walked toward them, slowly. He raised the shotgun to his shoulder just like Jason had shown him a thousand times, and pulled the trigger.

The shotgun's blast rang louder than most of the sounds flying through the air. The only thing louder was the pained scream of the Arkansas trooper as at least a dozen buckshot pellets penetrated his torso.

Methodically, Ricky pumped the action and took aim again. Three more times, he repeated the process until all of the attackers were down. A couple were still moving, but writhing in pain, and weren't much of a threat.

Jason hadn't even gotten a decent sight picture.

He looked at his son as the younger man turned to look at him. "Prisoners?"

Still in shock, he nodded.

Ricky nodded his acknowledgement as he put more shells into the shotgun. "I'll go get the doc."

"He's got his hands busy. Find a couple of people to carry them to the triage point."

Ricky laughed. "Might be better if I just finished them now in that case."

Jason looked at his son quizzically.

"The last couple we took over there? There's not much left of them now. People are pissed."

He could understand that.

Another trooper burst through the trees, about twenty yards from Jason.

The report from the 9mm pistol blended with the blast from the shotgun, both hitting the man and crumpling him into a pile on the blood-soaked ground. The two men - Jason couldn't look at Ricky as anything but a man now - looked at one another.

"Where's the militia?"

"Probably dead. Billy said he sent riders for you and Hector as soon as that attack was over, but it's kept going."

Jason jerked his head toward the town. "Go. Someone's got to keep people safe. I've got your mom and sister covered." He'd been gone when all this happened. It was time he started trying to keep himself home more.

Ricky nodded and trotted off, weapon at the ready.

Chapter 7

This was a first for Ricky. His father had taught him to shoot as a way to defend the homestead while he was gone, but to take the fight to the enemy? This was definitely a new experience in a week full of them.

Ricky tried to talk to his father about the first man he'd killed. All he'd said was he was most upset about how he wasn't upset. His father grew up in a world where killing wasn't generally accepted, though self defense was a little different.

In contrast, Ricky grew up in this world. Here, killing was still unfortunate, but it was also a way of life. He'd seen more dead bodies by his thirteenth birthday than professional morticians before the war had seen during their entire careers. At least, that's the way his father always phrased it. He had a different view of life and death than his dad had grown up with.

A woman's scream interrupted his ponderings. He changed direction and brought the shotgun up to his arm, keeping the barrel pointed down just like Dad had taught him. The screams came from behind one of the houses.

Dad had taught him how to go around a corner, swinging out wide and keeping the weapon at the ready. "Slicing the pie", he'd called it. Ricky just called it a smart tactics. Countless times doing it had been repetitive at the time, an annoyance. Now, Ricky did it automatically, his mind already shifted into a special place for this kind of work.

As he rounded the corner, Marla Monahan lay pinned on her back, several of the blackshirts held her down, one between her legs, struggling with her skirts. A couple yards behind them, Katie Miller stood defiantly, a bloody meat cleaver in her right hand. Several wounded or dead troopers lay near her feet. A half dozen others faced her, knives at the ready. Their guns lay piled next to the house.

"Come on, you bastards!" Katie screamed. "I've dealt with tougher than you pricks."

Ricky fought the urge to laugh. Everyone knew what Katie had endured. She'd started learning how not to be a victim again, but she hadn't been home all that long. He liked the attitude though.

No one had seen him yet. That gave him time. He carefully aimed at the man - no, trooper. *Best not to think of them as people.* He carefully aimed at the trooper between Marla's legs and fired.

The trooper's head exploded.

The element of surprise effectively gone, Ricky aimed at the next and fired. The trooper fell backward, his uniform torn to shreds. He worked the shotgun like a machine, pumping, aiming and firing almost as quickly as a semi-auto. At such a close range, he wasn't going to miss.

Now free of her attackers, Marla got up and ran. Tears streamed down her face as she sprinted past him.

Several troopers still partially surrounded Katie, but half of them turned to face the new threat behind them.

"Afternoon, gentlemen," Ricky said with a mischievous grin. "I don't think the lady's much interested in your attentions."

The troopers said nothing as they spread out in front of Ricky. There'd been no time to reload the shotgun, so he only had one shot left. *Who's the lucky one?*

Ricky wasn't built like his father. Where Jason was at best an average height, Ricky towered over most. Years of farm work had given him big, strong muscles compared to his father's wiry frame.

As he looked at the three troopers, only one compared to him physically. The trooper in the middle might have been a couple of inches shorter, but easily matched him in weight. Jason smiled at him for an instant before firing. The range was so close, the buckshot never had a chance to spread, all the pellets hitting the trooper square in the face.

Ricky quickly shifted his attention to the other two. He moved quickly toward his right, slamming the wooden butt of the Mossberg into one trooper's gut, then shifting toward the trooper to the left, slamming the butt of the weapon against his jaw. Years of watching militia butt stroke drills, then copying them with his father when Mom wasn't looking, paid off as the trooper collapsed.

The trooper recovered, a vicious snarl on his lips. "I'm gonna gut you like a fish, you fucking hick!"

Ricky smiled. "Bring it."

The trooper knew his business with a knife. While Ricky wasn't an expert, he'd seen plenty of them at work in his life. This guy was one. However, skill only could take one so far. Ricky had reach.

The trooper rushed him, trying to negate Ricky's advantage. Ricky was used to that. Smaller men usually tried to rush him in fights. He thrust the shotgun's butt into the other man's face, multiplying his own strength by the trooper's speed.

The trooper staggered back.

Ricky wasn't about to give him time to recover. He dropped the shotgun and closed. He grabbed the wrist holding the knife and twisted it, trying to get it out of the trooper's hand.

No longer stunned, the trooper began to punch at anything he thought would do damage. He guessed right on some as pain shot through Ricky's body as the troopers fist connected with a kidney.

Ricky held the troopers knife hand in place with one of his own, then slammed his elbow into the trooper's face. He turned his attention back to the knife and twisted again, this time toward the trooper's thumb. The knife tumbled to the ground.

Ricky slammed his elbow into the trooper's face again, then turned and punch him in the jaw as hard as he could manage.

The trooper staggered back, his face bleeding.

"You could always surrender," Ricky offered. The guy was good, and he was getting tired.

"Fuck you," the trooper growled back.

"Fair enough."

Suddenly, the trooper's eyes widened as his face slackened. He then dropped to his knees, staying there for a few moments before flopping forward, a meat cleaver embedded in the back of his head.

Katie Miller stood behind him. "Got tired of your jawin'," she said with a smile.

Ricky smiled back, then stood. "Thanks," he said as he began to reload his shotgun, the sounds of fighting still echoing through the town.

"Any time," she said.

Ricky turned to walk toward the sounds. After a few steps, he turned his head. "You coming?"

Katie smiled as she trotted after him.

** ** **

Jason stood on the porch, rifle at the read. There'd only been a few haphazard "attacks" since Ricky left to go into the town. It wasn't organized in the least.

Sounds from the town were slower now, more sporadic.

"Think Ricky will be back soon?" Jess asked from the doorway.

He nodded.

"Why did you send him?"

Jason sighed. He really didn't think now was the best time for an argument, but here it was.

She preempted him. "I'm not saying it was wrong or anything. I'm just curious."

He jerked his head toward the dead men in the field. "That's all him there."

"Really?"

He nodded. "He's one."

She cocked her head to the side. "Care to clarify?"

"He's like my dad was."

"Still not tracking."

"How do I explain it? You know those guys who were just fascinated with the military? Had been since they were kids, and even going off to war and seeing it up close didn't turn it off? Just about everyone grows up with someone like that."

She nodded.

"The way Dad explained it was there were people drawn to war and conflict. Sure, some of them were bad men who wanted to hurt people, but most weren't. They were warriors to the core. He used to say that there was a switch in each of us, but it was off. From time to time though, God would reach into the womb and flip it on. Used to say people like that were God's insurance policy, a way to make sure there were always experienced warriors ready to do His work."

"You believe that?"

He nodded.

"I guess you're one of those," she stated matter of factly.

He paused for a moment. "Didn't used to think so. Then the war happened."

She crossed her arms and leaned against the door frame. "Maybe your switch got flipped a little late?" she asked with a slight smile.

He shrugged. "Maybe. Who the hell knows?"

The sound of hooves caught his attention. He readied for the rifle and focused on keeping his breathing steady.

The first horseman came into sight and Jason relaxed. He often joked about shooting Billy, but never really saw the need most of the time.

Jason slung the rifle and walked out to meet him.

"How bad?" Jason asked.

"Bad," Billy said as he dismounted. "Not as bad is it could have been, but bad enough. About a hundred dead. Twice that wounded."

"Prisoners?"

"A few. For the record, Holliman surrendered first. Even killed a couple of his own guys before giving up his gun."

"We need to keep him safe. I hear folks

aren't too keen on keeping these boys alive."

"We're dealing with it."

"For the record, Jess had a prisoner before I even got home. He's in the house. Ricky got those over there," he said, pointing toward the tree line. He smiled. "Looks like they don't need me around here for much."

"Milton?"

"Nothing, but something's up over there."

"Oh?" he asked, raising an eyebrow.

Jason filled his friend in on all that had transpired during the visit with Milton.

"Damn," Billy said. "Connie left? Really?"

"Yeah. If you believe that, I've got some beachfront property in Kansas for you."

Billy laughed mirthlessly. "I bet."

Jason looked around. Sounds from the town now consisted solely of moaning from the wounded and screams of pain. "We need a damage assessment and I need a hard count on how many people are ready to go. We both know the council's going to have some questions."

Billy nodded.

"Also, try to send some scouts to their camp. If they're not there, I want to know where these assholes went."

"Consider it done."

** ** **

The days that followed were as chaotic as the attack had been, only a different kind of chaos. Homes needed to be rebuilt, wounds needed tending to, and plans needed to be made. It was learned quickly that the Hernandez family was missing. A townsman who had been visiting, a younger man named Caleb Jones, had been killed. Caleb had befriended Xander and was playing with the younger man.

They weren't the only ones missing either. At least fifteen other women were gone, most about the same age as Megan Hernandez, though a couple were younger.

Despite several days of rebuilding, Jason found himself standing outside of the council. Inside, the council was meeting to determine what, if anything, would be done. Several people had already stopped and asked him what was happening. He didn't have anything to tell them. Their guess was as good as his.

"Still nothing?" Jason jumped at the sound of his son's voice.

"Jesus! Don't sneak up on people like that."

Ricky shrugged. "Usually you're a bit more aware of what's going on around you."

"Yeah, I guess. I'm a little preoccupied right now."

"So, I guess that means there's still no news?"

Jason opened his mouth to answer, but the council building's door opening interrupted him. He turned as the council members filed out. John Mitchell looked at him for a moment and gave a pained smile before turning his gaze back and walking on. Simon was the last one out.

"So?" Jason asked.

"We're going."

"Figured. Who's commanding?" Jason asked. Most folks already knew the answer, and while Jason wasn't thrilled to do it, he also knew his reputation meant he couldn't really say no either. After all, that reputation is why everyone figured he'd be in command. That's why Simon's answer floored him.

"Daryl McDaniel."

"What?" Jason felt a confused mixture of relief and anger. He knew Daryl, and he was a nice enough guy. However, "nice" wasn't exactly the kind of criteria you needed to consider when declaring what was essentially war.

Simon shrugged. "Me and Mitchell wanted you. We got outvoted."

"Wow. Didn't see that one coming," he said softly, still in shock.

"Jason, I'm sorry. I really am. Unfortunately, McDaniel's been through the militia commander training, so he was qualified in the eyes of the council and he didn't manage to piss a bunch of them off not that long ago."

"Damn politics," Jason spat.

Simon shrugged again. "I know you hate it, but it's just how things work. Did before the war, does even now. We did manage to get you appointed as second in command. You've done rescues before, so they couldn't really say no to you being part of the command structure."

"If Daryl listens," Jason said. Daryl was a nice guy, but he was stubborn. Hell, for that matter, Jason was too, but this was different.

"Convince him. That's all you can do." Simon patted his friend on the shoulder before turning and walking off.

"When are we going?" Ricky said.

Jason shook his head. "You're not."

Rick's eyes widened, his mouth falling open.

"It's not like that," Jason said, knowing where his son's mind had run. He knew that Rick was already figuring that he was simply counting his son as a kid. "I'm getting a bad feeling about this. There might be an attack here after we leave. Get more of the women, whatever. I'd feel a hell of a lot better if you were here to make sure they didn't get a finger on your mother or Allison."

Ricky seemed to settle down after hearing that. "Still..."

Jason nodded. "Yeah, I know. It sucks. You did good. Never doubt that, alright?"

"Hey, Jason?" a voice called from behind him.

He turned, seeing Daryl McDaniel standing behind him. McDaniel was about Jason's height, but more roundly built, in his homemade overalls with, thinning brown hair and a round, smooth face. While no one was chubby right after the war and the ensuing winter, McDaniel packed on the extra pounds pretty quickly after the skies cleared and the food supply stabilized.

"I guess you heard?" the other man said.

Jason nodded. "I'm not sure whether to offer congratulations or condolences," he said, forcing a smile as he offered his hand.

McDaniel shook it. "Yeah, me neither. My wife ain't going to be thrilled, I can tell ya. Still, it's gotta be done."

He nodded. On that part, at least, he agreed completely. "Yeah. I've got some intel at the office if you want to come by later and take a look." He didn't want to mention that the "intel" was Al Holliman, unsure of whether anyone was listening.

"Thanks. I'll try and be by."

Jason nodded. Like it or not, this was his

commander and he couldn't *make* the guy talk to Holliman.

"How many are we talking there?" Jason asked.

"Not sure yet, but we can talk about it a little later. Maybe after I look at that intel you've got?"

Jason nodded, feeling a bit relieved. If McDaniel was going to look at the intel, it made sense to do that and then figure out what to take and who to leave behind.

"Well, I need to go break the news at home. I'll get with you before we head out, alright?"

"Sure," Jason said with a slight smile.

He watched as McDaniel walked off, unsure as to whether the swagger in the man's step was real or imagined.

** ** **

Jason was already home when Jess got back with Allison. The little girl darted for him the moment she made it through the door frame, a cry of "DADDY!" ripping through the air.

"There's my baby girl!" Jason leaned forward on his chair, his arms outstretched, waiting on the pile of energy barreling toward him.

Still barely in the house, Jess smiled as she

closed the door and walked toward the couch. Allison leapt into Jason's arms. He wrapped them around his daughter and pulled her onto his lap as she excitedly yammered on about her day. Jason nodded and smiled, asking questions from time to time about whatever subject she was talking about at that instant. The subjects flew from one to another in rapid fire succession.

Jason looked over at Jess, now sitting on the couch, and smiled. Allison wound the onslaught down, kissed him on the cheek, then hopped down and ran to her room.

"Seems like she had quite the day," he said.

She nodded. "And you?"

"Daryl McDaniel's commanding. I'm second."

Jess raised an eyebrow. "Really?"

He shrugged. "It's politics. I pissed them off at the last meeting, so now I'm being put in my place."

She shook her head. "Yeah, I mean, you've done this before. Heaven forbid you be trusted to do it again." Jason wondered if he needed to mop up the sarcasm that had spilled on the floor.

"Not my call," he sighed. "And I'm stuck. I have to go. If not, it's sour grapes that I'm not calling the shots."

"You don't think people around here are smart enough to figure out that you're not going because you value your life?"

Jason cocked his head and studied his wife. "Now come on. That's a little harsh. McDaniel's seen plenty of action. Hell, in this town, who hasn't?"

"Yeah, but it's all been defensive action. You said it yourself that there's a difference between fighting to defend a point and fighting to attack something."

"That doesn't mean he can't."

Jess flopped back on the couch, crossing her arms. "Who the hell are you trying to convince? Me or you?"

About to protest, he brought himself up short. Did she have a point? After all, he was the only possible commander who'd actually attacked something before. Sure, he'd been stupid as hell about it. His survival had been something of a miracle. The fact that it worked was beyond a miracle.

A pounding at the door snapped him from his thoughts. He got up and opened it.

"Sheriff, we need ya quick," a young man said, panting for air. He looked at Jason's naked hip. "You're gonna need your gun too," he said a moment before he ran off.

Jason sprinted back, grabbing his gun belt

off the table next to his chair, and took off after the young man.

** ** **

Ricky examined the group before him. Fifteen men, all armed in some way, shape, or form, looked back with murder in their eyes. He could see Billy and Hector being dragged out of harm's way. That left the him alone until his father could get there. *Come on, kid. I'm kind of on a deadline here,* he thought as he held the Glock G-17 in his right hand, finger on the trigger.

"Boy," said John Baskin, "There ain't no reason for you to get hurt. We just want the girl."

Ricky turned his head slightly. Katie Miller stood behind him, her meat cleaver in her hand. He had no doubt that one wrong move and John Baskin would be turned into bacon. Unfortunately, there were too many for her to handle alone.

"I kinda think she's of a different mind," Ricky said, a calmness in his voice that he didn't really feel anywhere else.

Baskin took a step forward in defiance.

The G-17 swung up, just a couple of feet from Baskin's face. "Back up," Ricky said, both hands holding onto the Glock like his father taught him all that time ago.

"You fool!" Baskin screamed, saliva flying from his mouth. "She is the reason for all this." He waved his hand toward the destruction around town square. "We must do right by God's will and purge her from our midst. She must be fed to the purifying fire."

"Mention 'fire' one more time, and I'm going to take it as an invitation." His hand was steady, though he couldn't figure out how that was happening for the life of him.

"Come on, boy," one of the other men said. He was a rough looking man, with stubble around his chin, a close hair cut, with a deep tan and slight wrinkles in the corner of his eyes. Ricky recognized him from the fields, but couldn't recall the man's name. "You can't think you can take us all. You've got fifteen shots in that gun. Tops."

"Seventeen. That means I can shoot a couple of you twice," he answered. His eyes zeroed in on Baskin, and he said, "or, I can just shoot your ass three times."

The rough man laughed. "You really think you're that badass?"

Ricky smiled. "You really want to take the chance that I'm not?"

"Baskin!" a voice Ricky knew well called out from the other side of the square.

All heads but Ricky's swung toward the new voice. Jason Calvin stood, his AK-47 pointed at the mob. "You really think this is a good idea?"

"We *will* purge the harlot from this town!"

Jason swung the AK up to his shoulder a split second after taking the safety off. "And I'll purge this town of a few less assholes. Put your weapons down."

The mob didn't move.

"Now!" he shouted.

Ricky watched carefully. He knew that if someone had the drop on him, this is when he would try something. Several men moved and Ricky tensed. He relaxed a few moments later when they laid their weapons on the ground and stepped back, their hands up.

"Everyone," Ricky said, in an icy tone.

"Fuck you, boy," Baskin spat, bringing up the revolver in his hands.

That was all Ricky was waiting for. He squeezed the trigger, sending the 9mm round rifling out the barrel, easily clearing the two feet or so between the end of the barrel and John Baskin's left eye.

As if it were a starting gun, the other armed men, most of whom already had their weapons trained on someone, began firing. Bits of clay pelted the back of Ricky's head as bullets struck the wall behind him. Instinctively, Ricky shrunk down, trying to make himself as small a target as humanly possible.

Out of the corner of his eye, Ricky saw his father walking forward, the AK firing round after round. Ricky's Glock was working just as hard as he focused on the front site of the pistol and squeezed the trigger when it lined up with his target. Adrenaline coursed through his body, shutting out the loud reports of the weapons. BLAM! BLAM! The rough looking man took two rounds to the chest, but was still standing. He raised his weapon toward Ricky, who stroked the trigger one more time.

The rough man fell to his knees. He looked down for an instant before falling forward.

Ricky swung the gun to the next man. It was Quinton Elias. He and Quinton hadn't gotten along. Apparently, the older man didn't appreciate being told how to do his job by a kid. Ricky had no hard feelings from the event, but the evil grin on the other man's face said the feeling wasn't reciprocated.

Quinton fired a shot. It slammed into the wall where Ricky stood just a moment before.

Ricky knew the Elais was more dangerous than most of the others here, so he grabbed Katie with his left hand and urged her forward. One handed, he fired at the man. His first two rounds missed, impacting harmlessly on the ground at the other man's feet.

Quinton returned fire, doing no better against the moving targets. Unfortunately for him, he was too focused on Ricky until the moment a 7.62x39mm round punched through his chest a split second before Ricky's one handed shot slammed into his right shoulder.

Quinton Elias died before he hit the ground. The thud from him hitting the hard Tennessee dirt the only sound in the now deserted square.

Chapter 8

Jason and Simon walked through the town square turned battlefield. Bodies of the would-be mob littered the ground. Out of the fifteen original, ten were dead while two more had been injured and quit the fight. Three had backed off, and weren't harmed.

Anyone involved who wasn't in the hospital building were locked up in the jail that was suddenly feeling rather cramped.

"Damn," Simon said as he looked down at John Baskin's body. "Didn't think he'd be crazy enough to try this crap."

Jason shrugged. "Well, apparently he was. He was also stupid enough to think Rick wouldn't pull the trigger." He looked over at his son.

Ricky stood to the side of the square, one arm wrapped around Katie Miller. For the first time since before she had disappeared, the blonde was smiling. Her attention was squarely on Ricky, who had a nervous smile of his own.

"Yeah, well, that was clearly a mistake," Simon said.

"You think?"

Simon smiled. "He going with you?"

Jason shook his head. "Nope.

The chairman considered that for a moment, then said, "I'm not quite sure how I feel about that. No offense, but he's got some serious skills."

Nodding, Jason said, "Yeah, that he does. Not what I wanted for him when he was born, but whatever. The world had different plans. But I've got a bad feeling about this thing we're about to do, and I'd just as soon he be around after."

"You don't think Daryl can hack it?"

He shrugged. "I'm not sure. I mean, he's never done anything like this, but I hadn't either when I did it the first time." He paused, considering what he really wanted to say. "I guess it's the fact that you and I know this is based on politics and nothing else."

"It's like I said. Everything is politics."

"Yeah, I know. But I also know what happens when politics starts trying to fight wars. Vietnam was screwed from the start. Iraq went to shit the moment we left. Russia started shit and next thing you know, we're dodging mushroom clouds. A whole damn history of politicians screwing up and other people dying over it."

"So what? You want the militia to determine when to go to war?"

Jason shook his head. "Nope. But that's where politics should stop. Once the decision is made, they need to get the hell out of the way."

"No one is telling McDaniel how to fight this. You know that, right?"

Jason laughed. "You really think Cory Masters isn't going to try and put his fingers in this?"

"Yeah, actually, I do. Cory's an idiot, but he's not that big of an idiot. He knows he'd be bounced off the council if we even suspect he'd pulled anything like that." Simon stepped in front of Jason, putting himself face to face with his old friend. "It's not perfect. Probably never will be, but it's not as bad as you think."

Jason smiled. "Yeah, you're probably right. I've just had a lot on my mind."

Simon nodded. "Fair enough. What about your guys?"

"They're alright. One of them had a taser. Put them down, but nothing permanent."

"Good. Are they going to be able to hold down the fort while you're gone?"

Jason nodded. "Billy's scarier than I am. Hector too. Both of them know what to do in most any circumstances they're likely to encounter, and they've done it enough that I'm not worried."

"Good."

He nodded in agreement with Simon's assessment. If only he could shake that feeling.

** ** **

Terry Conklin sat back in his air conditioned office, enjoying his return to civilization. He couldn't help but think about how those Tennessee hillbillies had been going all Little House on the Prairie with their tech base. *Losers*. He didn't plan on correcting them either.

It was late in the day. Plaques and trophies, the mementos of a bygone era, littered the walls and shelves. Those things had once meant so much to him. Now? He knew they didn't mean much in the grand scheme of things. Appearances, however, must be maintained, and commanding officers always have their "love me" walls.

His desk was an antique, a work of woodcraft mastery, complete with baroque carvings and beautifully forged pulls. He almost felt bad for putting his feet up on such a beautiful work of art. Almost.

Conklin leaned back in his chair and did just that an instant before a knock at the door sounded through the deep blue painted room.

"Yeah?" he bellowed.

The door opened. Ramirez entered.

"We've got them all in holding," he said.

Conklin nodded. "Good. Megan Hernandez?"

"She's down below, sir."

He smiled. He had no illusions about how feral he looked, so he forgave his subordinate for the shudder. At least the man had the good grace to try and hide it. "Good. Leave her down there for a few days. Minimal rations."

Ramirez nodded. "Yes, sir. And the New Eden women?"

"I need a few days. I don't want to bring them up all on the same charges. Appearances and all that. Plus, there are the other reasons for keeping them around, so I'm not even sure we're going to indenture them."

The subordinate nodded.

"What is it?"

"Are they coming?"

Conklin laughed. "You really have to ask that? Did you look at their sheriff?"

The other man nodded. "Yes, sir, but I got the impression that he doesn't call the shots."

"Of course not. But I'll tell you one thing. That man? He's the only worthy son of a bitch I've run into since the damn war. He'll come. Even if he's by himself, he'll come."

Ramirez looked puzzled. "How do you

know that, sir?" His eyes flew open wide as he said, "Not that I'm doubting you, sir. I'm just curious."

Conklin smiled. Oh, the Army had tried to say that good leaders took care of their men, but he'd since learned that fear worked better than hippy bullshit ever would.

"Because, Major Ramirez, that man is a crusader. He's got the Itch. He'll come, and he'll fight. Too bad for him he's an amateur."

Ramirez nodded. He'd gotten the intel on Jason Calvin's life story, so there were no questions on that front.

Oh, Conklin was duly impressed with what Calvin had accomplished since the war, but he'd bumbled his way around. Conklin, on the other hand, was a pro. He'd been trained by the best on tactics and strategy.

"He'll come," he continued, more for himself than his man's benefit. "He'll come, and then we'll unleash hell on Earth."

** ** **

Just days had passed since the gunfight in town square. Now, he found himself on the road, walking with the dismounted militia. That was fine with him, since he wasn't much of a horseman in the first place.

What did bother him was Daryl McDaniel repeatedly dodging him to discuss intelligence. *What the hell kind of commander doesn't try to learn as much about the enemy and their defenses as possible?*

"So, Jason? What's the plan when we get there?" asked the man walking next to him.

"You'll know when you need to know. Don't sweat it right now." Jason wasn't an expert on leadership or anything, but he'd learned enough to know that that these men needed to believe in their leadership. Telling them that he didn't have a damn clue wasn't really the best way to go about making sure that was the case.

Hours droned by, the monotony of walking for hours on hard, broken asphalt failing to help the time speed by in any meaningful way. All around him, men played ridiculous car games, made even more ridiculous by the slow speed of their passing. I Spy was fine at forty-five miles per hour, but at a walk? Damn boring.

When the order passed to make camp, Jason was relieved. While the pace had been relatively mild, his mind turned the seemingly endless miles through the dense trees torturous.

Tents dotted the relatively flat area. The only way Jason could describe the formation of tents was absolute chaos. He'd stopped at several tents, only to find they weren't the right

119

ones. Exasperated, he finally yelled, "Anyone know where Commander McDaniel is?"

One of the militia members directed him toward the western edge of the encampment. Sure enough, the militia commander was there. Outside of his tent, a fly had been set up. Beneath it, a small wooden knockdown table sat with several chairs around it. McDaniel looked at a piece of paper with one of his aides.

The militia commander looked up and smiled as Jason approached. "There you are. I was wondering where you'd gotten off to."

Jason fought the urge to roll his eyes. "Well, considering how the camp's set up, it's a freaking miracle I found you at all."

McDaniel shrugged. "I know, but I was never a big fan of that crap when I was in the Army. Never saw where it accomplished a damn thing."

"Well, it would have helped me find you for one."

The other man smiled. "You're here now. That's what matters."

Jason turned his attention on the aide. "I need a minute with the commander. Alone."

The aide look at Jason, his contempt for the sheriff obvious.

"Go away," Jason growled.

McDaniel dismissed the aide with a nod, his

friendly demeanor now gone. "No need to be rude, you know?"

Jason shrugged. "Hey, I tried to be polite. He didn't get the hint."

McDaniel smiled again. "True enough. What can I do for you?" he asked as he motioned toward a chair on the opposite side of the table.

"Maybe you can tell me what the hell the plan is?" Jason asked as he stepped forward, pulled out a chair and sat down.

"We're working on it. We don't have a lot of intelligence."

Jason laughed mirthlessly. "I had intelligence sitting in one of my cells, but you didn't seem interested."

"Yes, well...I had been briefed that the turncoat wasn't reliable."

"Really? That's funny. Who told you that?"

"I'm not at liberty to say."

"Oh, you don't have to 'say'. I know who the hell told you, and if we even survive to get back, I'm going to nail his ass to the wall."

"There's no need to get upset. We'll assess the situation when we get there and plan accordingly."

Jason shook his head in exasperation.

"Is there a problem?" McDaniel asked.

"Yeah, there is. You could have talked to

my guy, gotten a briefing on the layout, and at least had some idea what the hell was going on. Instead, we're going to go in blind and hope we can figure out where the hell everyone is."

"We've both been through the militia commander training. The first step is to assess the threat, and we *will* do that before any plans are in place."

Jason stood up. "And you assess a threat using all available information, including human intelligence when available, as well as your on site assessment. Did you forget that part?" he asked, then turned and walked away.

** ** **

"Uh, Mrs. Calvin?" said a familiar sounding voice. Jess turned carefully, trying her best not to bump into anyone in the crowded market.

Katie Miller wove her way through the bustling crowd and smiled. "Can you talk for a minute?" she asked.

Jess nodded. "Sure. Just call me Jess, Okay? I'm still not comfortable with being called Mrs. Calvin or anything," she said, adding a smile at the end.

The other woman smiled back. "Um...I'm not really sure how to say this."

"Well, I'd go with as simply and directly as you can. I'm a big girl. I'm sure I can take it," she said, flashing a quick smile.

"Okay. Um…I was just wondering if Rick had a favorite food or something? I'd really like to invite him for supper one night and…well…I want it to be something he'll enjoy."

Jess wondered when this was going to happen. Jason told her about how their son stood up to an angry mob, defending the girl. She wasn't sure quite how she felt, but she also knew it wasn't her decision.

"Well, his favorite food is Jason's spaghetti sauce, but that's a family secret," she said, with a smile. "Next would probably be fried pork chops."

The other woman smiled. "Any sides he likes…or doesn't like, maybe?"

"Steer clear of peas. It's not that he doesn't like 'em. He's allergic. It's not fatal or anything, but unpleasant for him."

Katie nodded. "No peas. Got it," she said, then spun on her heels. After a few steps away, she turned part way and said, "Are we still having class tomorrow?"

Jess nodded. "Absolutely."

"Good. I appreciate what Rick did and all, but I'm not crazy about needing help."

She stepped forward and put her hand on the younger woman's shoulder. "Darling, in case you missed it, Ricky needed a little help too. No shame in it from time to time. Just don't be needing it on a regular basis."

She nodded. "Yes, ma'am. I understand that. Unfortunately, it's the second time he's done it. Helped me that is."

Jess nodded again. "I heard. The thing is, you're not interested in being a victim, right?"

The younger woman nodded.

"Good. Ask Ricky to teach you how to shoot if you don't know already. Keep coming to class. Learn everything you can. Everyone needs protecting at some point in their lives. Maybe next time, you'll be protecting him."

Katie nodded, a broad smile stretched across her face. "Yes, ma'am. I like the sounds of that pretty good."

** ** **

Days had worn on as the militia made its way through the Tennessee mountains. Somerton was finally in sight.

Anxiety flooded through Jason as he looked down at what had once supposedly been a tiny community at the foot of the mountains. Now, it sprawled out in all directions.

In the core of the town were the pre-war buildings. Brick and wood sided structures sat side by side along carefully laid out streets. A small park appeared to still be well maintained.

Outside of the core, however, was a whole different world. Whereas New Eden had learned how to build houses without the supporting infrastructure of the pre-war world, Somerton had instead resorted to what could charitably be called shacks.

Mismatched pieces of plywood, nailed to old pallets or anything else that could give them structure, formed the bulk of the walls for these outer buildings. The roofs had once been car hoods, now overlapping one another like shingles. Rusted sheet metal ran along the peaks of the roofs, trying to bridge the gap between the two sides.

Slowly, the "army" made its way down through the thick vegetation. Fields of wheat butted up to the tree line and ran the entire quarter mile to the edge of town with a single "road" running through the middle of it.

Jason stood his position, trying to hide the sense of dread that had only grown since his talk with McDaniel.

The militia commander hadn't indicated any hard feelings, and been downright amiable every time Jason had talked to him. However, he also hadn't included Jason in on any of the planning for his operation.

Probably shouldn't have blown up like that at the

briefing, Jason thought. *Then again, it's not like I had a lot of choice. Someone had to say something.*

Jason's job was to command the reserves. He'd been instructed to only deploy them with explicit orders, and he'd acknowledge those orders.

McDaniel and the cavalry burst out of the tree line on a dead run, pushing their animals as hard as they could toward Somerton.

So far, so good, Jason thought. He wanted to be wrong about all this, and prayed that McDaniel was right. The distinct lack of gunfire was a good sign.

In the middle of town, a church bell clanged its warning. Something like this had been expected, so none of the militia was concerned.

Suddenly, a roll of thundering gunfire erupted from the wheat fields on either side of the charge. Dozens of men fell from their horses. Another half dozen or so did their best to keep from being crushed as their horses collapsed beneath them.

Shit!

"All elements, stand by for orders," Jason called out as the roar of the enemy guns continued. *Where the hell are you, you little bastards,* he thought, scanning the wheat to get an idea of where the Somerton troops were. Oh, he knew they were on the flanks, but there was still nothing to shoot at.

Jason watched as McDaniel wheeled this cavalry to face the oncoming threat, forming one line each facing the side. *Come on, Daryl. Get the hell out of there.*

The cavalry troops fired down on the Somerton infantry. Jason prayed they had a better view of the enemy than he did, because otherwise they were just shooting wheat.

More and more of the New Eden cavalry fell. Men he'd known for years dropped like flies.

Infantry began pouring out of the fields, their focus on the cavalry. Dozens of men clogged the narrow road. *At least I have something to fight!*

"Infantry, open fire!" he bellowed. In an instant, he was rewarded with the booming reports of New Eden rifles.

The first wave of shots slammed into the Somerton troops like a hammer smashing a porcelain vase, leaving only a thin line between the cavalry and the safety of the tree line.

Come on! Punch through! Jason couldn't believe what he was watching as still more of his friends and neighbors fell to enemy gunfire. Somerton troops filled in where his men had opened up the possibility of retreat. Worse still, they knew the reserves were there and were shooting back now.

Fuck orders.

He turned to find the Cavalry reserve commander a few feet away. "Max? Take your men and hit them from the North. Punch a hole through to our guys. Meet up at rally point delta."

Max nodded and sprinted toward his horse, mounting it with inhuman speed. Jason knew that the man had heard not to deploy without orders, but only an idiot would follow that order now.

Jason quickly assessed the lay of the land, trying to formulate a plan. Somerton troops were now peeking up from the wheat, their black uniforms striking against the golden crop. His quick estimate was there were a butt load of them, and this was *not* going to end well.

"First and third squads!"

The commanders of those squads nodded. "Ben, take your men North as far as you can and still see these assholes on the road. Then lay on fire as hard as you can. Sam, you go South and do the same."

Both men nodded, then spun on their heels and ran back to their men. Jason watched for just a moment to make sure his orders were being followed, then swung his attention back to the chaos in front.

The Somerton troops were catching the worst end of the deal with their current exchange, but they also had a lot more people.

Jason's, on the other hand, at least had some cover and plenty of concealment from which to fire on the black-clad enemy. Not enough, as his own men were dropping far more often than he was comfortable with, but some.

He brought his own rifle up and joined his own fire to that of his men. "Just another day in the park, boys!" he yelled, an evil grin crossing his face. His voice held more confidence than he actually felt, but that was another of those facts he knew about leadership.

Now, if he could just get enough of his troops out alive.

** ** **

Conklin watched the battle through binoculars. Ramirez was calling the shots down below, and from what Conklin could tell, doing a hell of a job.

He looked at the enemy, finally dropping off their horses and using the big animals as cover. He checked each face, desperate to find one person in particular.

A chubby looking man with thinning hair

seemed to be the one giving the orders, not Calvin. *What the fuck? Where the fuck is Calvin?* Conklin wasn't used to disappointed these days.

He continued to scan the battlefield. Some of his men were firing toward the trees. Casualties along that front were much higher as well. *There's the bastard. Hiding in the trees. And to think I considered you worthy.*

The group in the midst of the ambush was dwindling quickly. They'd soon be wiped out, then Ramirez could turn his attention toward the tree line. *Then I'll own you,* he thought as an evil smile crossed his face.

"Sir?" a voice asked. Conklin sighed.

"What?"

"I'm sorry to interrupt, but these need your signatures right away." Conklin turned and studied the intruder. Short, skinny with a bulging Adam's apple, and beady eyes, he was the kind of guy Conklin would have dragged into a bathroom and flushed his head in a toilet back in high school. Unfortunately, people like that had their uses, and he'd learned to use them just fine.

He considered a moment. His first impulse was to send the man out, probably throw something just for the hell of it. Then again, it looked like Ramirez had everything well in hand.

"Put 'em on the desk. I'll get to them in a

minute."

The man nodded a split second before Conklin turned his attention back to the battle. It was annoying that, of all the things to be lost in the war that bureaucracy wasn't one of them.

A flicker of motion out of the corner of Conklin's eye caught his attention. He brought his binoculars up and watched. *Heh. I guess Ramirez should have seen that one coming.*

** ** **

A chorus of ear piercing screams cut through the gunfire, jerking Jason's attention away from the enemy in front. Accompanying the screams was the rolling thunder of horse hooves ripping up the ground beneath them.

"Watch your shots," Jason shouted.

The cavalry reserves fired their pistols into the mostly unaware infantry in the northernmost field, their bullets like scythes reaping the dead. Those not killed by bullets were soon trampled by the four legged onslaught thundering down upon them.

Jason turned his attention back toward the infantry in front of him. The fight was almost monotonous at this point. He'd done everything he could think to do. Now, it was just killing. He'd found out through the years he was good at that.

From man to man, he settled the front site of the AK on a black uniform and squeezed the trigger. Adrenaline coursing through him, washing away the fear that should have consumed each man present.

Horses darted into his field of vision, staying his trigger finger. Enough of his people were dead as it was. The last thing they needed was blue on blue to top a perfectly bad day.

He shifted to a target south of where his relief force had smashed into the enemy. It was still a target rich environment, after all.

Round after round rocked the AK against his shoulder. Methodically he hunted down the men in black, ending them without remorse. No matter how many he and his people killed, however, there seemed to be more of the black-clad bastards to take their place.

Reluctantly, he lowered his rifle just a bit, enough so he could focus on the relief force. Max was in the saddle, helping men up on their. Others were being pulled onto already occupied horses.

"Keep 'em focused on us!" he bellowed, bringing the ancient rifle back up and firing again.

Mere moments. That's all it really took for Max's men to break through, gather the survivors, and begin their breakout. Jason knew it had just been moments with every piece of intellect he could muster.

It didn't matter.

Those mere moments stretched on for an eternity. Jason held his breath until Max and his men had completed the maneuver and were heading well away from harm.

"Alright," he muttered. Too many littered the field beyond the enemy, but a lot more were still alive. He grabbed a man by the shirt, pulling the other man closer. "Tell First Squad to pull back one hundred yards and hold."

The man nodded and ran toward First Squad in the north. Jason grabbed another. "Send Second Squad three hundred yards back." The militiaman seemed confused. "Go!" Jason ordered. He didn't need the man to understand the whys of the order, he just had to repeat it.

Fire from the north slowly trickled off a few minutes before the gunfire slacked from the south.

"Alright, here's the plan," he said as loudly as he dared. "We're done, but I'll be damned if these bastards run us all the way back to New Eden. When I give the order, we roll back. No one runs for it. We pull back, but we fight our way back. Everyone got it?"

Men nodded between shots, determined to

keep the pressure up on the enemy. Easier said than done now that they had only one threat to worry about.

Fire in their direction intensified exponentially. *Enough of this shit.* "Okay, pull back," he called out.

Slowly, methodically, the militia moved back, firing at the battered enemy. Wounded men limped back as best they could, or found themselves being carried by their brethren. Unfortunately, there was no options for the dead.

Jason hated it. He hated the idea of leaving anyone behind. It wasn't in his nature, it was damn sure not what his father had practically beaten into him. However, no one lived this long in this world without having a strong pragmatic streak. Carrying the dead would get more people killed. No way around it. Especially since most of them were surrounded by the enemy.

When the retreating force hit the hundred yard mark, First Squad held the line. "Hold here until we're all past, then fall back another four hundred yards, got it?"

The First Squad commander nodded.

The militia slowly wove their way through the thick underbrush. Pursuit seemed to be slowing, but Jason wasn't taking any chances.

Walking in the woods is relaxing for some people, but those folks have never had to deal with an army intent on wiping you off of the face of the Earth also occupying the forest. Instead, the ragtag survivors jumped at every sound like skittish game.

For whatever reason, the pursuit had stopped.

Chapter 9

Conklin sat at his desk. Across from him, Ramirez stood, ramrod straight. The younger man's anxiety could be felt in the air.

"So, you failed to account for additional forces," Conklin said.

Ramirez nodded. "Yes, sir. I did. No excuse, sir."

"Body count?"

"Eighty-three, sir."

"Wounded?"

"Forty-six, sir."

"Enemy dead?"

Ramirez stood a little taller as he spoke, "Four hundred seventeen."

"Make no mistake, major. You fucked up," said, enjoying the other man's discomfort like a connoisseur with a fine Pinot Noir. "However," he continued, "you successfully defended the city and defeated the enemy in detail. Your mistake was the only hiccup in an otherwise excellent job."

"Thank you, sir," Ramirez.

"How many survived?"

"Unknown, sir. We didn't get a clear indication of how many held in reserves, so any estimate I give will be simply a guess." That was why Conklin liked the man. No bullshit, just a straight forward, honest answer.

"They pulled their own wounded?"

"Yes, sir."

"Commendable."

Ramirez said nothing. Conklin may have give his subordinate a vote of confidence, but he also knew that he'd trained the younger man well.

"I think we need to prepare a message for our friends in New Eden. Let's make sure Zulu Company is part of the festivities this time."

A malicious smile crossed the subordinate's face. "Yes, sir. It'll be my pleasure."

** ** **

Jason looked at the troops, the sullen faces looking back at him. They'd had their asses handed to them, and no one enjoyed that. It was a sharp contrast to the group that headed out just under a week ago.

He'd chosen this rally point because it was where the supply wagons had been left, along with a small compliment of men to guard them. Those men, confident of a successful mission, looked more dumbfounded than the survivors did.

Daryl McDaniel wasn't among the survivors.

"Sir?" a voice said, tearing him away from his own thoughts and bringing him back to the small clearing near an old state highway along the eastern side of a mountain.

Jason looked at Ben Richards, who'd commanded First Squad. "Sorry," he said.

Ben nodded. Jason knew they were all taken aback by what had happened to some extent or another.

"Alright, here's the deal. We've got wounded, and we're still too damn close to the enemy. We're going to have to load them up in the wagons and get moving."

Ben nodded again, this time more sullenly. Jason wasn't surprised, and couldn't say he blamed the other man either. They were tired and the sun was inching closer toward the horizon. That meant moving through the night.

Jason understood that, and really wanted nothing more than a good night's sleep, though he was sure sleep wasn't remotely possible. Unfortunately, what they wanted happened to be irrelevant.

Carefully, men began placing the dismounted wounded in the wagons where ever they could find space. Those wounded who could ride or walk, did.

A third, if that. That's all we've got left. His mind wandered home, already dreading the reception when they got back.

Once the wounded were fully loaded, they began the long, winding journey home. For the first twenty-four hours, they moved for as long as the infantry could manage, then stopped for only as long as necessary.

Jason sent mounted scouts forward as well as behind him, anything he could do to warn of any possible ambush. One per week was plenty for him.

After the first twenty-four hours, there were still no signs of pursuit. Jason called a halt and ordered the infantry to rest. The cavalry, he put on the first watch, but on foot.

Ben Richards approached him as he sat on a tree stump. "We got a plan?"

Jason shrugged. "Get home. Alive"

Richard squatted down, resting his forearms on his knees as he fiddled with a pinecone. "That sounds like one we can live with."

"That's the plan."

"I've got to ask though. What the hell happened?"

Jason looked around. He saw no one in earshot.

"I could tell you, but frankly I'd rather not

139

speak ill of the dead until I don't have a choice."

Ben nodded. "Figured it was something like that."

"You and Daryl were friends, right?"

He nodded again.

"Did he talk to you about why he shut me out?"

He shrugged. "Not really. Saw him doing it though. A lot of us did. Figured he didn't want you taking over or something."

Jason shook his head. "For what it's worth? Trying to keep stuff tight to the vest so you're indispensible? Never works the way you want."

The other man chuckled. "Yeah, unless you're a medieval guild." Ben had been in college, studying history with hopes to get a PhD in medieval history. He never missed an opportunity to talk about the Middle Ages.

Jason shrugged. "Maybe, but they still shared it with plenty of folks. They just made sure everyone was vested in keeping quiet. One craftsman wasn't indespensible, because there were plenty of other craftsmen who knew the same stuff."

"That's fair," Ben said with a sad smile. He and Jason chatted about medieval history from time to time.

"I wonder what all we lost," Jason said, his eyes starting to look at the dense forest around him.

"You need numbers?"

Jason refocused on the other man. "No. I know those. Not what I meant though," he said, then let his eyes drift again. "I wonder what all we lost as far as knowledge. We're trying to piece a world back together. That's what New Eden's supposed to be about."

"Well, I know we lost Dave Jenkins." Jenkins was a tinsmith extraordinaire and not half bad with precious metals like gold and silver.

"Damn," Jason said, dropping his gaze to the ground by his feet. "I always like Dave."

"Everyone did. He was one of those guys."
** ** **

The battered troops staggered into town a week later. By that point, no one was riding unless there was absolutely no choice about it. Jason didn't know a lot about horses, but he knew they were living beings and that he could only push them so far.

As they passed the outlying farms, kids sprinted toward town, all hoping to be the first to announce the militia's return. Passing by the people of New Eden, people who had already experienced so much pain and privation, now looked on at friends and neighbors who'd just had a whole new taste. A defeated army has a very distinct look, and everyone picked it up.

A mass of bodies lined the road leading toward the town square by the time the militia got there. Sad eyes scanned the remnants, desperate for the sight of a loved one.

Jason did his best to hold his head up, to look people in the eye. Some of them had lost someone they cared about. Hell, most of them had. The least he owed them was to be acknowledged.

The militia finally wound its way through town and into the town square. Across the square, the council waited outside the council building.

"Dismissed," Jason called over his shoulder. The men had been through enough. There wasn't any reason to drag it out even further.

Jason made his way across the square, his eyes locked on the council.

When he finally got close enough, Cory Masters blurted, "What the hell happened?"

"Inside," was all that Jason said.

"I want to know what the hell happened! Answer me!"

Jason stepped closer toward the building, stopping just beside Masters. "I fucking said inside," he growled.

The councilman jumped at the tone, his

eyes widening as he looked at his fellow council members for support.

Jason entered the council building, the council members filing in behind him. The click of the door was a signal. Jason spun and grabbed Cory Masters with both hands and slammed him against the door.

"What the hell!" the councilman yelped, his anxious eyes darting from side to side.

"You! You, you little fuck!" Jason growled, using all of his self control to not rip the council member into pieces.

"What are you talking about?" he asked Jason, then looked at the other council members. His allies stood in slack-jawed shock. Simon and Mitchell watched, arms crossed. "Aren't you all going to do something?"

"Of course they aren't. I'm willing to bet they're pretty interested to hear how you interfered with the militia."

Simon's arms dropped as he stepped forward. "That's pretty serious. Are you sure?"

Jason nodded. "Daryl didn't bother to talk to Holliman. Best intelligence we had, and he didn't come to ask him any questions. None."

Masters struggled at Jason's arms, doing his best to break the vice like grip. "That was his decision. I didn't have anything to do with that!"

"Yeah? Then how come he said he'd been

told the intelligence wasn't reliable? Only my two guys and the people in this room knew about Holliman. That's it, and my guys believe him."

"You're nuts!"

"I just watched over four hundred of our people get slaughtered. You're damn right I am." Jason said, his eyes growing more wild with each word.

"Jason," Simon said. "You need to put him down."

"What I really need to do is take those four hundred dead out of his ass."

Master's eyes grew about four sizes as a puddle formed on the floor. "No...no...please...I didn't mean anything, really. I just-"

"Shut up!" Jason yelled, small drops of saliva sailing through the mere inches between the two men's faces.

"Put him down, Jason. I mean it."

Jason dropped the man, who immediately collapsed on the floor, oblivious to the fact he was sitting in his own urine.

"What happened?"

"McDaniel didn't talk to Holliman, so he didn't know what Somerton's capabilities were. Then he fucked up and didn't do any meaningful recon."

"Really?"

Jason nodded and took a deep breath. He forced the rage that consumed him down, but didn't dare even look at Cory Masters.

In as much detail as he could muster, he recounted the days leading up to the battle, and the battle itself. When he'd finished, the council members stood in various states of disbelief.

"I didn't...that's not what he was supposed to do," Masters said.

"What the hell did you think was gonna happen, boy?" John Mitchell barked. "You're his buddy on the council. You say something like that, what the hell did you think he was gonna do? Ignore you? You son of a bitch. You might as well have put a gun to his head and pulled the damn trigger."

Jason nodded. "Yeah, he wasn't. But McDaniel should have reconned Somerton better. Should have tried to figure out what was going on there, capabilities, the works"

"Did he know that Conklin had over two thousand troops with him when he was here?"

Jason shrugged. "I offered to share my intel with him, but he passed. I assumed the council had briefed him."

"You!" Masters blurted. "You should have made sure he knew! Then you come in here, blaming it all on me?"

"Shut up!" Mildred Evans screamed. "I'm tired of you and your ridiculous notions. I'm absolutely sick of them."

Stunned eyes settled on the woman, normally so quiet and preferring to work behind the scenes to make things happen.

Evans continued, "I looked at every face that came back. Did you? Do you even care? One of the faces that left but didn't come back was my grandson. You, you sanctimonious piece of shit, tell a militia commander something like that, and they take it as gospel. You either knew that, in which case, you're responsible for all of those dead, or you didn't, in which case you're a complete idiot."

Evans turned her attention to Jason. There was no love lost between the two, mostly because Evans had this idea that all of her ideas of morality should be enforced as law, and Jason strongly disagreed. "As for you, Sheriff Calvin, do you honestly believe that Daryl McDaniel would have listened to you if you'd told him the reported troop strength?"

Jason shook his head. "No, ma'am, I don't."

"Are you still kicking yourself in the rear? If we need a scapegoat, I think Masters will do nicely, but I'd rather avoid that. The truth is, I voted for Daryl because of personal differences with the sheriff and not because I thought Daryl was the best man for the job."

She held her hands up defensively, then continued, "Now, I thought he could do it, so I'm not saying I really didn't think he was capable. I'm just saying he wasn't the best."

Jason nodded. In fact, he'd thought McDaniel was capable as well. Truth was, had Masters kept his mouth shut, he might have done just fine. No one would ever know for certain, however.

"Jason?" Simon said. "Can you step outside? We've got some council business to discuss."

Jason nodded. Based on what had just happened, he knew what was going to happen. Cory Masters wasn't going to be much of a problem any longer.

He considered for a moment before nodding his head. That very thing had been in the back of his mind from the moment he'd been able to focus on something other than not being killed.

** ** **

Conklin picked his way carefully down the old staircase. The ancient town hall's basement had never been high on the list of priorities when time for remodeling came up. The rickety stairs, even less so. Not that Conklin was particularly picky. The fact was, the difficulty in getting down was more of a feature than a bug.

Rotted furniture, a thick blanket of dust covering them, created an obstacle course along the concrete floor. More dust floated through the air like a swarm of bugs in a summer meadow.

Conklin negotiated the course with the ease brought about by repetition.

A closed steel door with a small diamond shaped window brought him up short. Conklin peered through the glass, black lines crisscrossing the pane. The single bulb dangling in the hallway cast light too dim to penetrate the darkness on the other side of the door.

He reached into his pocket, pulled out a key and unlocked the door. Stepping in, he flipped the switch by the door.

Another dim bulb hung just inches from the ceiling, too high to reach without a ladder. Despite the poor light, the room's occupant squinted. He wasn't surprised by that. In fact, he counted on it.

This was his domain. Megan Hernandez wasn't the first he'd put in this room. She wouldn't be the last, either. He had a pattern for the women he brought down here, and it served him well.

This time, things were different though. Rather than cowering in the corner, Megan Hernandez stood. Her arms were shackled and chained, so her mobility was next to nothing, but she still was standing.

"What are you going to do?" she said, her voice still strong.

Conklin felt the rage growing within. It's bad enough that she wasn't as terrified as she was supposed to be, but worse that she dared speak.

SLAM! The back of Conklin's hand connected with Megan's face, spinning the woman around.

That'll teach the little bitch, he thought, as a vicious smile crossed his face.

Megan turned to face him. Slowly. A murderous glint in her eye, she stood upright once again.

The rage grew within him. Didn't this stupid bitch know who he was? Of course she did. She'd run away from him, so she was scared. She had to be.

Still, this was definitely not fear he was looking at.

"Oh, you've got some fire? I like that. It makes breaking you even sweeter," he said, forcing his voice to remain calm despite the seething fury within him.

"You ain't seen shit yet," she said, drawing herself up a bit taller.

Conklin smiled malevolently. "You talk a big game for a bitch chained to the floor, you know that?"

"Yeah, well, it helps that you fucked with the wrong town. You really think they're going to let this stand?"

"Actually, I do," he said.

"If it'd just been us, maybe. But their own?"

Conklin laughed, then threw a right cross that connected with her cheek. "You stupid cunt," he said, no hint of humor left in his voice. "Oh, they tried. We've got the bodies burning outside of town right now. They tried, and they were slaughtered."

He threw another backhand, this time connecting with the other cheek. "Hell, coming for you girls might have killed their entire pathetic town."

"I don't believe you."

Conklin shrugged, the rage growing exponentially. It was harder to feign calm. "That's alright. We're arranging a little surprise that should do a fine job of driving the point home that they'd best leave well enough alone."

It was her turn to laugh, the melodious sound fueling the rage even more. "I talked to a lot of folks about those people. You really think Jason Calvin listens to messages?"

He smiled, this time it was genuine. "He'll get this one."

** ** **

Al Hollimon sat across the table from Jason. The last two days had been spent with memorial services. Reverend Hardesty had been busy, but so had Jason. Memorial services for over four hundred people, and funerals for three of the wounded that hadn't made it tended to draw on your time.

The room wasn't anything special. Whitewashed walls amplified what little light leaked in through barred windows. The desk was basic in design, as were the chairs. An oil lamp sat on the desk between the two men.

"Alright, tell me everything," he said to the Somerton man.

The other man raised a single eyebrow. "Um, where do I start?"

"Start with Conklin. Give me his story."

Holliman nodded. "Conklin came to town right after the war. He was in command of an Army unit that showed up about three months after everything went to shit."

Jason nodded. "Deserters?"

"From what I understand, lots."

Jason remembered the stories. After the war, the military effectively didn't exist. No government left to call the shots meant no one to give the military orders.

Some units did what they could, while others went raider. The raider units tended to have high desertion rates, since most people really didn't want to kill innocent people just over some food.

"Then?"

"To start with, he seemed like a decent enough sort. Offered to help protect the town in exchange for some food. We'd been holding out, but the raiders were getting stronger so we weren't sure how long we could keep doing that, so we took him up on it."

Jason nodded. It wasn't unusual, even for the "good" units to make similar offers to small towns. A few of them made homes a bit further up the valley, as a matter of fact.

"I've got to ask you a question though," Holliman said.

Jason raised an eyebrow in response.

"You going back?"

He nodded. "Waiting on the official go ahead. They're 'discussing' it at the moment."

"And if you don't get it?"

"Then I'm going anyways, but I'm probably

out of a job when I get back."

Holliman smiled. "A man after my own heart."

"I'm glad you think so, because you're going to come with me."

"Oh?"

Holliman had been holed up in the jail most of the time since Somerton's raid, so Jason filled him in on the failed rescue. Holliman shook his head.

"That's a damn shame," the resistance member said. "We could have helped. We'd have loved to have helped."

"You'll get your chance."

Holliman nodded. "Good."

Jason was about to speak when a knock on the door interrupted him.

He got up and opened the door. Billy stood outside. "Boss, we've got something outside. You need to see it."

Jason nodded, then turned to Holliman. "You stay here." He didn't wait for a response before following his friend out the room.

Billy sprinted down the rough stairs, his long, powerful legs eating up the ground beneath him. Jason's shorter legs meant he had to sprint even harder just to keep pace.

As he exited the building, a mass of people were moving toward the town square, as was

Billy.

Jason wove his way through the growing throng until he finally saw what the commotion was all about.

In the middle of the square stood a horse. While Jason didn't know much about horses, he knew this thing would barely qualify for any description like "old nag" and not even come close for anything better. The horse pulled a worn cart. The cart had some kind of load, a load covered by a thick brown tarp.

The council, minus Cory Masters, stood near the back of the cart, John Mitchell standing with an arm around a sobbing Mildred Evans.

Simon turned as Jason approached.

"What's up?" Jason asked.

The chairman simply nodded toward the cart.

Jason peered at Simon quizzically, then turned his attention toward the cart. He stepped forward and pulled up the tarp.

Beneath it were the heads of the New Eden dead. Several he recognized, but just barely, including Daryl McDaniel.

Bile rose in his throat as he fought the urge to vomit. He'd seen a decapitated head before. Hell, he'd decapitated a man himself, almost a decade earlier. It wasn't a new experience.

This was different.

Jason turned to a townsman, one he knew had a way with animals. "Get this out of here, will you?"

The man nodded, then stepped forward to take the horse.

Jason directed him to a place just outside of town and asked him to hold it there for a little while.

He then turned to the council. "We need a work party. They deserve a proper burial, but we just don't have the time to dig all those graves."

Simon nodded. He began to speak when an odd whistling sound pierced through the air.

Joe Campbell, who'd done several tours in Iraq, started screaming. "Everyone, down!" a second before a loud explosion rocked the south end of town.

Another whistle, another explosion. This was to the north. Jason knew they were being bracketed.

The only weapon he had was the CZ in his holster, which wouldn't be enough to deal with Somerton troops, but he had to do something.

He wasn't an expert on mortars, but had read a handful of things about them. One thing he knew was that they fired at a very high angle. That meant they used a clearing, and one not too far away.

Only one place fit the bill as far as he could tell.

As he ran, he screamed, "Get to the shelters!"

The town had dozens of deep storm shelters. Joe had helped design them to withstand artillery to some extent, figuring that if it could take near misses by massive cannons, then a tornado wouldn't be too devastating.

Around him, chaos ensued. Billy caught up to him easily, a pump action shotgun in his hand.

The rounds were falling faster, the whistling sound preceding them giving too little warning. Explosions caused the very ground to shake as people bolted for shelters, often running the opposite direction from the closest one.

A mortar round screamed through the air, the noise getting louder as it approached. Jason screeched to a halt, grabbing Billy in the process as the big man tried to continue on.

Just a moment later, one of the houses erupted as a round landed on it. Debris flew in all directions as the shockwave pushed it forward. As the wave slammed into the two men, it lifted them off the ground, throwing them several yards away.

Fighting to remain conscious, Jason looked over at Billy. The big man was already out, but he noticed his chest rising and falling. *He's alive,* Jason thought as darkness clouded his vision.

** ** **

"Jason?"

He heard Hector's voice, calling to him through the darkness.

"If this is heaven, I expected Rita Heyworth or Kate Beckinsale to be the one to meet me," Jason said, his voice sounding groggy to his own ears.

Hector laughed.

Jason forced his eyes open. His head throbbed as the world came into focus. "And if this *is* heaven, I want my money back."

Slowly, he pushed himself up. "Billy?"

Hector nodded. "He's alright. Tameka took him home a little while ago."

"She probably blames me for this. She's always saying I'm a bad influence." Jason shook his head, trying to shake the cobwebs free. He was rewarded with an increase in the headache's intensity.

"How bad?"

"Mostly structural, as best we can tell. Most folks are still in the shelters."

Jason nodded, instantly regretting it. "Jess?"

"Haven't seen her."

157

That surprised him. Oh, he figured she wouldn't worry about him, necessarily, but Allison was at the school and who knew where Rick was. And there were a lot of other people. Jess fussed over people.

"Help me up," he said.

The big man reached down, taking an arm and pulling his boss up. Jason's head pounded at the movement, but he wasn't really interested in caring about that right now.

His first steps were tentative, like a new foal fresh into the world. With each successive step, he felt steadier and steadier. Soon, he found himself running, his head making its displeasure known.

Behind him, he could hear Hector following. The big man wasn't nearly as fast as Billy, which made him only as fast as Jason. Right now though, one of them was a bit more motivated than the other.

Jason ran down the deserted roads until he rounded the bend closest to his house.

He stopped, shocked.

The house, or what was left of it, was spread out all over the place. The blasted remains of trees littered the ground. All around the remains, that ground looked more like the lunar surface than the Tennessee Valley.

"Jess?" he yelled.

Nothing.

Hector caught up to him, panting like a south Georgia dog in August.

Jason paid little attention to his friend as he bolted toward what was left of the house. Hector, despite his obvious fatigue, followed.

"Jess?" He screamed, hoping she would answer, praying that she couldn't because she was in one of the shelters.

Shards of dried mud and straw covered the floor of his home, little of it could be seen. Jason grabbed the closest piece and threw it outside of what little wall still stood.

To his right, Hector mimicked the action.

Jason's head throbbed worse and worse with each movement. He didn't care. It didn't matter. Nothing mattered except finding Jess.

His armed burned. Each piece was heavier than the last. Small pieces weighed a ton. Each lift powered more and more by will than muscle.

A flash of white caught Jason's eye as he lifted another piece. He remembered Jess wearing her white blouse that morning.

"Hector!" he called.

The deputy rushed over, the two lifting pieces, trying to pull her out.

A flutter caught his eye. Was she alive?

He attacked the pile with renewed strength. "ARGH!" he grunted as he and Hector lifted the last piece, a massive hunk, and tossed it to the side.

Chapter 10

Rick pushed his way through the crowd. The tightly packed shelter was stifling. He was desperate to get out and taste fresh air again. Running and hiding wasn't something he particularly relished.

Katie Miller stood beside him, her body still pressed close, despite the newfound freedom. Not that he minded. Not really.

He looked around for any of his family. He knew Allison was in school, and would stay there for a while even after they got out of the shelters. His father, on the other hand, had to be there somewhere.

All around, people were asking questions. How many are dead? Anyone hurt? Was their house okay? What about the school? Ricky listened, but he didn't have any answers either.

He heard a gasp above the din of the crowd. Heads all around shifted to the northwest. Ricky couldn't quite see what the commotion was.

Katie apparently could.

"Oh God!" she gasped as she began to cry.

Rick looked down at her, ready to comfort the girl. She was looking up at him.

He swung his head back toward the commotion. He still couldn't see. He took a step. Not much, just enough to get Hoss Tompkins from between him and whatever it was that everyone was staring at.

Walking down the road was his father, Hector a few feet behind him. In his arms was the limp form of the woman who'd given Rick and his sister life.

"No. No, can't be," he muttered.

"I'm so sorry," Katie said through her tears. The girl was tough. She had to be after what she went through. He knew that, yet tears streamed down her face. The truth was, he wasn't sure he didn't need it.

He forced his feet to move toward his father. Katie walked with him, but his notice of her began to fade.

With each step, his hopes began to dwindle. The closer he got, the easier it was to see his father's face. Sorrow and rage battled across the man's face, neither giving up ground.

Rick knew his own face was a similar battlefield. The difference was, right now, rage was winning and he was fine with that.

Standing just a couple feet from his father, Rick watched the man drop to his knees, his mother's limp form dangling.

The boulder in his gut seemed to grow. A

prickling sensation tickled his face. Rage ripped through him, fueled by the pain of seeing his mother lying before him. A quick look at his father told him the feeling was mutual.

Jess Calvin was going to heaven. Rick and Jason were going to make sure the train to hell was packed.

** ** **

Days passed in a fog. Jason barely remembered anything. Much of the town had come to see him. Any lingering resentment over his survival of the ambush seemed gone.

Jason and Rick nodded politely, smiled painfully, thanked them for their kind words, and promptly forgot who said what. He only barely remembered Simon telling him about a note beneath the heads stating that the girls currently being held would be killed if New Eden launched any further attacks.

The two of them sat around the table in the parsonage. Reverend Hardesty offered it until their home could be rebuilt. What was left of their furniture was stored in various barns around the community. Allison was in school. It was her first day back after the loss of her mother.

Jason remembered how he had to break the

news to his daughter. So young, but she'd taken it better than he had. The young were resilient, and the young in this world even more so. That's not to say she wasn't upset. What kid wouldn't be. She was just handling it as well as anyone else could in this day and age.

A knock on the door drew his attention. It opened, a creaking noise filling the air. "Can I come in?" asked Reverend Hardesty, peeking in through the opening.

Jason smiled as best he could and nodded.

Hardesty entered the room. His overall were coated in dirt. He'd been an avid gardener before the war, a pastime that continued for very different reasons after it.

The old man pulled a chair and helped himself. "How you boys holding up?"

Jason shrugged. "How well can we?"

Hardesty nodded.

Rick's eyes remained focused on the table by his clenched hands. His knuckles had turned white.

"I know you're talking about going back to Somerton," Hardest said. Jason liked the old man's bluntness.

Jason nodded. It's not like it was particularly secret, especially right now. Everyone expected it.

"You doing this for the right reasons?"

Jason shrugged. "Maybe. I don't know. Right now, I don't care."

"You remember what the Good Book says? 'Vengeance is mine, sayeth the Lord' and all that?"

He nodded. "I remember it."

Hardesty breathed deeply, the corners of his mouth threatening to turn up in a smile.

"I also remember what Genghis Khan said."

The old man looked at Jason, a questioning eyebrow raised.

"I am the punishment of God...If you had not committed great sins, God would not have sent a punishment like me upon you," he said, his voice deepening.

"That's not your place to decide. You know me well enough by not to know I'm not one of those 'love everyone and let them kill ya' type preachers, but I'm worried about this path you're looking going down."

"They've still got fifteen of our people. Plus, I told the Hernandez family that I'd do everything I could to protect them. I said that in this very room."

Hardesty nodded. "You think I don't know that, boy? And it's not that you want to free our people that bothers me."

"Then what is bothering you?" Rick asked,

anger filling his voice.

Jason fought back the urge to tell his son to show some respect. He knew who the anger was for, and it wasn't for the preacher.

Hardesty swallowed hard before he spoke. "I'm worried that you're going to be so focused on revenge that you'll forget what's important."

Rick looked up. Calm. The icy calm that seemed to have washed over his oldest chilled Jason to the bone.

"Vengeance belongs to God. So be it. I'm volunteering to be the instrument of that vengeance. In the process, I don't just want Conklin dead. I want everything he stood for, every evil he built, every wrong he committed to be crushed beneath my boot. I want him and those like him to tremble at the thought of what awaits them should they ever try to hurt us again."

Slowly, the younger man stood up.

"Reverend. You're a good man. You were built for the old world, and managed to survive in this one without losing your soul. Good for you. Me? I'm not. Dad? Well, you'll have to ask him, but I know I'm not. I'm the Angel of Death, and Terry Conklin is about to find me on his doorstep."

The young man stood up and walked out.

Jason cleared his throat a few seconds after

the door closed behind his son. "Sorry about that. The boy can be a bit dramatic." He smiled, a smile as genuine as he can manage.

Hardesty nodded. "He is at that," he said with a smile.

"Doesn't make him necessarily wrong, either."

The old man shook his head. Jason held up a hand, stopping him before he could respond. "I'm just saying that I agree with him about beating Conklin. Live. Die. That's irrelevant. Beating him? Making it so he knows that he failed? From what I can tell, *that* is how you get revenge on someone like Conklin."

"So you're not just planning on taking the man's life?"

"Of course not. Rick'll see that as well. He just needs time to calm down. That's all."

Hardesty nodded. "Okay, if you say so." He pushed himself up from the table. "Well, I need to see some other folks today. You know where to find me if you need me," he said with a smile.

Jason stood up and smiled. "Of course. And I appreciate you stopping by. I really do."

Hardesty walked toward the door, Jason right beside him.

The two men stepped through the door and out into a beautiful Tennessee afternoon. Rick leaned against a tree, defiant.

Jason bid his farewells to the pastor, then walked up to his son.

"Did I miss much?" Rick asked, sounding more like a seventeen year old with attitude than he ever had before.

"Yep. Missed me telling him that we're not going there with any intention to kill Conklin."

Rick laughed, his anger tainting any mirth in it. "Speak for yourself."

Jason's eyes were still on the pastor. "You need to learn a little tact. It can come in handy from time to time."

"Not my strong suit. Besides, didn't you manage to piss off the entire council a time or two?"

He nodded. Rick was more of a direct and blunt sort. "Well, I said you need to learn it. Not that I could teach it." He continued, "besides, it's not like it was true."

Rick's gaze flew toward his father. "What?"

"Oh, we're going there and we *will* get our people, but we're going to kill the shit out of Terry Conklin, and for once, I'm actually going to enjoy it."

** ** **

Jason was in the office early. He had a lot to think about, and he'd done plenty of thinking here. In his hands were a stack of papers. Old, but still in good shape, they crinkled when he moved.

"Whatcha got there?" Hector asked.

Jason jumped, completely unaware Billy and come in.

"Nothing really. Just something I wrote up a few years back."

Hector raised his eyebrow, questioningly. "You're a writer?"

Jason smiled. "Used to be. Folks wanted me to write up what happened to me right after the war."

"Springing Jess?" Hector knew it had to be a sore subject, but he wanted to make sure.

"That, and getting there in the first place."

Hector knew the story. Most folks did.

"Never knew you wrote down what really happened."

Jason nodded.

"Mind if I read it sometime?"

"I thought everyone already knew what happened."

Hector shook his head. "Nope. We know the stories, but that's different. Things tend to get bigger in the telling. You know how they go."

Jason nodded. "Yeah, folks do tend to exaggerate, don't they?"

"What else are they supposed to do since they can't get into arguments on Twitter anymore?"

He smiled. "Fair enough." He considered for a second. "And yeah, feel free to read it any time you want. I'd rather you knew the truth as I saw it than whatever else is getting spread around."

"Cool. So…why are you reading it now?"

Jason shrugged. "Damned if I know. I just…I don't know. I guess it's just something about a time when I actually could do something to save her."

"You can't beat yourself up over this, man. You just can't."

He nodded. "Yeah, I know, but you've got to know that's easier said than done. After so much, and she died like that?" He shook his head slowly. "I'm always going to feel like it's partially my fault."

"Stop being a pussy," another voice said from the door.

Jason looked up to see Billy's hulking form darkening the doorway. "Who are you calling a pussy? And shouldn't your ass be in bed?"

"I'm calling *you* a pussy, and I'm not in bed because I'm not a pussy and didn't see a reason to stay home."

"Fair enough."

Billy hobbled in. He'd injured his leg in the mortar blast in addition to the concussion that knocked him out. The doc told him to stay in bed for another week. Of course, Jason couldn't criticize him too much. It's not like he'd have stayed in bed either.

"When are you going?" Billy asked.

Jason shrugged. "Trying to work it out. Been talking to Holliman, getting the layout of the town, the inhabitants, stuff like that."

Billy nodded. "Then focus on that. Stop with this blaming yourself shit. You and I both know it's bullshit."

Jason shrugged. Like I said, it's easier said than done."

"Do or do not. There is no try," the big man said with a grin. "Just make sure before you leave, you stop by here."

"Did you just go there? And why do I need to come here?" Jason asked.

"Yes, I did, and Hector and I'll have some surprises ready for you."

"It's good to be loved, you know that?"

"Yeah, but in a strictly non-prison movie sense," the big man said, holding his hands up as if to keep Jason away.

"Whatever helps you sleep at night," Jason said, feeling a bit better than he had in some time.

Chapter 11

Jason, Rick, Hector and Holliman snuck out in the middle of the night. So far as most anyone knew, they'd headed south to visit Jess's mother outside of Rome, leaving Allison with Simon's family while he was gone. In the context, it made perfect sense. Hector and Billy knew, of course. So did the council. The rest of town knew nothing. It was better that way.

Three of the men had worn backpacks put together by Hector and Billy. Hector had a bag with some essentials, but he wasn't going the whole way. After all, he was just going to relay some basic info back to New Eden. From the outside, there was nothing extraordinary about them, just regular old pre-war backpacking packs.

Rick and Jason both carried AR-15's, and carried about twelve hundred rounds each in the packs, along with food, some spare clothes, and what Billy simply called "surprises". Holliman opted to go unarmed, stating that if they happened to be captured, he could always claim to be a prisoner and get them out. If he happened to be armed, he didn't figure anyone was stupid enough to buy that.

Well, Jason was pretty sure Cory Masters would, but since he wasn't here, it wasn't worth worrying about.

Jason questioned that amount of ammo, however, since Sully told him there was a lot less. Hector admitted to having hit up some of the residents for extra. He didn't tell them why, just that he needed it.

The ammo made the packs heavy as hell, and then there was the food. They weren't taking a direct route to Somerton. That way was suicide. Instead, they had to come at Conklin from an angle. To do that, they needed to arrange a meeting.

That meant Milton.

Jason tried to shake off the last meeting with the man, but it kept nagging at him. Milton wasn't exactly a young man. Was it something about old age that was affecting him?

By early afternoon, Milton's home was in sight. The old man, now clean shaven, stood on the porch waving his arms over his head and yelling.

Jason started jogging at first, then burst into a faster run. Everyone easily kept pace.

As they got close enough, they could hear what Milton was yelling. "Hector! I need you, my boy. You're the doctor, and that's what I need."

Hector shifted into a full sprint, his long, muscled legs covering the distance in mere moments.

"Hector's a doctor?" Holliman asked.

"Graduated med school about two weeks before the war. Won't do more than emergency stuff though. Says it's because he didn't do residency and all that."

Holliman shrugged as they continued on.

Jason and company weren't far behind the big man, but Milton paid them no attention. As soon as Hector got to the door, the old man ushered him into the house and out of sight.

Jason stopped outside the house. "Rick, I need you to keep an eye out here. Something's not right, so be careful, alright?"

The younger man nodded.

When Jason got inside, he saw Connie laid on the living room couch. She'd been savagely beaten. Hector knelt beside her, already examining her.

"Who did this," Jason said, his blood boiling enough that he no longer was worried about what kind of man he was.

"This asshole named Conklin. He showed up a few weeks ago, looking for some family. I didn't know anything about them. He took Connie with him and left two of his people to keep an eye on me. Said she'd be alright if I cooperated and tell anyone who asked that I didn't know anything about what was going on in Somerton."

"I take it you did."

Milton nodded. "Of course I know. Who do you think you're talking to? I'm wired into every state in the continental U.S. Well, what's left of it, anyways. I think it's fair to say that D.C. was wiped off the map. Never have gotten a signal from there."

"So you knew who Conklin was?"

"Not at first. No visuals on radio transmissions, you know. But when he said his name, I knew exactly who it was. Oh, indeed I did."

"Well, that explains my last trip here," Jason muttered.

"I'm sorry about that, I really am. I couldn't tell you anything directly, but I wanted to try and let you know something wasn't right. That's why I was acting so out of it."

Jason smiled slightly. "Milton, my man, with you, it's easy to miss signals like that, you know?"

Milton shrugged. "It's the best I had."

Hector examined Connie as best he could. "I think she'll be OK so long as we keep fluids in her."

"I've been using a washcloth to help her

drink," Milton said.

Nodding, Hector said, "Good. Keep doing that until she can do it herself."

"Milton," Jason interrupted. "What about your radio? Is it still good to go?"

"Those two bimbos they left here trashed it before they left to go with their friends," he said, the grinned slyly. "Damn good thing they don't know about my backup."

"Backup?"

"Oh, hell yes. Got a radio shack hidden. Did it just in case someone ever got froggy about coming up this way."

Jason smiled. "Nice. We need it."

"Oh?"

Holliman stepped forward. "Yes, sir. I need to call some folks back in Somerton and let them know I'm coming home and bringing a whole mess of trouble for Conklin."

Milton's sly smile shifted into something with far more malevolence. "Oh, well, in that case, wait here. I've got most of the replacement components here in the house. Just got to grab the last couple of things, and we'll be ready to go later today."

"Beautiful," Jason said.

"One thing though, Jason my boy."

"Oh?"

"Make him pay for hurting Connie."

"Oh, don't worry. We will."

** ** **

The men moved Connie to the bedroom where she would be more comfortable. She wasn't out of the woods yet, but as close as she could be with what they had to work with, or so Hector had said.

They sat in the living room. Holliman made his call. Everything was set. Jason excused himself and stepped outside.

A light rain fell, the drops beating a soothing rhythm on the lush canopy. He'd always had a soft spot for rain. Before the war, a rain storm was an excuse to step out to the porch and listen to the sounds.

Luckily, Milton had a large porch.

"Sneaking away, my boy?" Milton said.

Jason smiled. "Something like that."

"We've known each other a long time, haven't we, my boy?"

He nodded. "Yeah, I guess we have," Jason said with a smile.

"What's bothering you?"

"You mean besides my wife being killed?"

"Actually, my boy, I do."

Jason glared at the older man. "Who says anything's wrong?"

"Like you've already agreed, we've known each other a long time. You're carrying a lot of guilt at the moment. Anyone who's known you a while can tell."

"Then how come no one's said anything?" Jason replied. He could feel his face burning as he clinched his fists, his fingernails cutting into the palms.

"Oh, my boy, any number of reasons. Oh yes, any number of reasons indeed."

"Such as?"

"I don't know. Each man's reasons are his own, and no man owes me an explanation to someone like me." He sat down in a chair next to where Jason parked his rear. "It's also possible that none of them realize that it's about more than your wife."

Jason considered it for a moment. The old man kind of had a point. He'd felt guilty for the attack, but Jess being there had made it bearable. Without her? Wasn't going to happen.

"What happened?" Milton asked.

Jason laid out the whole story. He'd told it so many times, he was getting pretty good at it. This time, however, he didn't bother pulling punches about the mistakes he knew McDaniel was making.

Through it all, Milton sat and listened. He nodded most of the time, stopping occasionally to ask Jason a question for clarification.

When Jason finished, Milton looked at him. "Well, my boy, it sounds like you screwed the pooch royally."

Jason rolled his eyes. "Thanks, Milton. I really appreciate that. With friends like you, who needs enemas, right?"

"Don't you mean enemies?"

Jason shook his head and smiled. "Nope."

Milton smiled. "The fun thing is, no matter what happened? I'd have probably gotten to say the same thing."

"How do you figure?"

"You were in a bad situation, my boy. Anyone with half a brain could see that. You weren't in charge, so it wasn't your call, even though you *knew* this McDaniel fellow was wrong. On the other hand, if you'd have done something to take command, what would have happened? Well, it's possible the men's loyalty would have been tested beyond the breaking point, and when you actually made a move, it would have been worse."

Milton propped his feet on a small stool, built in a similar style to the chairs they occupied. "You're dealing with hindsight, my boy. Of course you're going to know the exact course you should have taken *now*. The problem is, you're not making the decision in this moment, but back then when things were still murky."

Jason nodded. It was true, but it didn't alleviate the guilt he felt. "You realize that doesn't actually make me feel better."

"Of course not. Men died, my boy. Oh, they died indeed, but you have to realize that whether it was your mistake or not, it's irrelevant. If it was your mistake, learn from it. If it wasn't, then move on and quit beating yourself up over it."

He laughed. "When did you become Yoda?"

Milton smiled. "How do you know I wasn't the basis for him in the first place?"

Jason's smile vanished as his eyes widened. Milton was originally from Southern California, and with his money, it wasn't out of the realm of possibility that he'd known George Lucas.

It was Milton's turn to laugh. "I'm kidding, my boy. Oh, you're such a gullible mark, you know that?"

He turned serious again. "We've know each other for a while, but have I ever told you what I used to do for a living?"

Jason considered for a moment. "Figured you were some kind of computer programmer or something."

Milton shook his head. "Nope. I was a

venture capitalist, believe it or not."

"Really?"

"Yep. As for why I know these things, it's because I had to accept them myself. Years ago, a few years before the war actually, I'd helped a young company start up. It was going well, and we got an offer from a much bigger company. Mid eight figures. That kind of thing.

"Well, we sold it. We thought the bigger company would just absorb it. Everyone did. The employees hated to see the bosses leave, but were pretty stoked about working for the big dog. Most of them anyways." Milton sat there, silent.

"And?" Jason asked.

"They laid everyone off. Three hundred employees. And this was during a recession, so there weren't other jobs left. Severance packages sucked too.

"I felt pretty guilty for a while. After all, the guys who started the company? They were technicians. I was the business mind. They were trusting me to steer them right. I blew it. Frankly, I beat myself up over it for a while too."

"So what did you do?"

Milton looked at him and smiled. "I just moved on. The next company we sold, I made sure there was a stipulation that the employees had to be in place for eighteen months. I wanted two years, but took what I could get. There were still layoffs after that time expired, but a lot of them stayed on too."

Milton put a comforting hand on Jason's shoulder. "The thing is, learn from what happened, but don't let it tear you up. You do that, you're no good to anyone. You won't avenge you wife, my boy, and you won't make them pay for what they did to my Connie. Oh no, you won't. All you'll do is be another notch in Conklin's belt."

Jason nodded. Much as he hated to admit it, the old man made some sense.

** ** **

Plans were finalized. It was time to go. Hector had already left, taking a handheld radio with him toward New Eden. Normally, Milton was reluctant to let any of his gear leave his possession, but once Hector mentioned that he could have gotten to Connie earlier had we known, the old man couldn't move fast enough to grab a handheld.

Jason, Rick, and Holliman headed out a different way. Milton knew his property was being watched. He had the bastards on camera, so he knew exactly where they were. He could only imagine that there were guards watching New Eden as well.

"So, how do we want to do this," Rick asks as they walked across the poorly manicured yard back in the direction of New Eden.

"We know where they're at, and we could use a bit more info. I say we pay them a little visit."

Rick's malevolent grin would have chilled Jason to the bone...if he hadn't had a matching one of his own.

Once safely hidden by the surrounding forest, Jason pulled out Billy's "surprise" that was wrapped in a burlap bag. Jason pulled it out, his grin growing even wider.

He quickly affixed the black suppressor to his AR-15 and showed Rick how to do the same.

Jason instructed Holliman to wait there while he and Rick worked their way through the dense brush toward the location Milton said his camera was situated. A slow pace was made even slower as the two men carefully picked their way through the brambles and brush.

Jason felt like hours had passed while they worked their way through nature's obstacle course, but he didn't worry too much about it. Time wasn't their most pressing concern right then.

Rick walked ahead of him, his rifle at the read. He threw up his right fist, motioning to stop.

Carefully, Jason worked his way toward his son. "Whatcha got?" he whispered.

The younger man nodded forward. Jason look, seeing three men in Somerton black.

"You're the better long gun shooter," Rick whispered.

Jason nodded and brought his rifle to his shoulder. The shot wasn't particularly long, just inside of a hundred yards, but the wind was starting to pick up. In all his shooting before the war, long distance precision shooting hadn't been something he'd worried about. Classes like that dealt with adjusting for the wind. Instead, he'd focused on learning how to shoot people in the face when he could actually *see* that face.

Well, it's always a good time to experience new things, I guess.

Jason looked down the ACOG scope. They were tough and reliable, but old. Luckily, they just dimmed with age and he could still aim just fine.

He knew the key would be to take at least one down where no one would know. Jason settled in for a long wait.

Several minutes passed when one of the Somerton men stood and walked away. Jason trailed him, keeping the scope on him as he wove his own way through the trees.

Taking a leak. Tsk, tsk. Sucks when you do that and don't realize what's around you. Poor situational awareness can kill ya.

The man stood with his back to Jason. As he unzipped his pants, Jason carefully squeezed the trigger.

The suppressor muffled the sound of the 5.56 round as he flew through the air, a supersonic crack the only noise marking its travel.

THWACK.

The round slammed into the back of the Somerton man's head, a red mist painting the tree in had been standing in front of just a moment earlier.

Jason swung the rifle toward the observation post. The two remaining men had apparently heard the crack of the round as it broke the speed of sound, but had no clue what they'd heard. Jason put on a predatory grin as he settled the ACOG's retacle on the next man.

Based on the man's body language, Jason figured he was in charge. There was the possibility of taking this man prisoner, as he likely had some valuable intelligence. Of course, Jason had Holliman, so he was covered on intelligence. Besides, and really more importantly, he didn't see any reason why the enemy would surrender.

Another squeeze of the trigger sent another round down range. The man collapsed right where he was.

That leaves one.

Jason scanned the general area of the OP, desperate to find the remaining soldier. *Great. The bastard figured out what was going on. Just not my day, is it?*

"We've got you surrounded," Rick called out. Jason looked up, meeting his son's eye. The younger man winked and grinned. Rick went back to looking at the OP. "Surrender now, and you'll be treated fairly."

A blond head popped up. "Fuck you!" he yelled defiantly.

"Fair enough," Jason muttered as he aimed and squeezed the trigger a third time.

** ** **

Rick went to fetch Holliman while Jason checked the bodies. A radio was there, but he saw no evidence of it having been used since it was still sitting in a pouch on the "leader's" belt.

"Find anything?" Rick asked as he approached.

"Radio."

"Nice. That should keep you in the loop on whatever Conklin's got going on," Holliman said.

"He always use the same channel?" Jason asked.

Holliman shook his head. "Nah. He uses a few, but that radio should access all of them"

"Good. I'll be damned if I go in blind again."

Rick grinned. "Maybe it'll tell us where to find his ass when we get there. Make taking him out a simple matter."

Jason turned to Holliman. "How much range does one of these have?"

"Few miles, tops. Why?"

"Didn't look like the last guy down made a move for it. I wondered why. Guess he knew it didn't have the range."

Holliman nodded. "Most likely. Probably had it for communicating with relief or extraction teams."

"When would they show up?" Rick asked.

Holliman shook his head. "No clue. It varies based on the mission. Hell, they might have just had a set time period to keep an eye on stuff here"

Rick cursed under his breath. "They're going to know we're coming."

Jason shook his head. "Doubtful."

The younger man peered at his father quizzically.

"It's still kind of the Wild West out here. Towns tend to be safe, but the spaces between? They're No Man's Land. People get zapped all the time. We just need to hide the bodies."

Holliman raised his hand, as if asking a question in school. "Um, what about Milton? Why wouldn't they hit his place?"

Jason smiled. "If there aren't bodies here, they won't know when they were hit."

"And if they're supposed to wait for relief?"

"Bad things happen. Milton's smart. He'll think of something to tell them. Probably something better than we'd come up with."

The two men nodded.

"Alright, boys," Jason said, forcing his voice to sound more confident than he felt. "We've got a long damn way to go, and we've eaten a lot of daylight. Let's get a move on."

The three men moved out, heading west by northwest, rather than making a beeline toward Conklin and Somerton.

Chapter 12

The small settlement before them consisted of pre-war houses, all neatly arranged around a looping road and surrounded by a brick wall. An iron gate, more ornamental than functional, provided the only easy access in and out of what Jason figured was a housing development.

As the three men approached the gate, an old sign welcomed them to Warrington Manor.

Holliman noticed Jason's gaze and laughed.

"Yeah, that's what they called this place before the war. Not so much now."

"Oh?" Rick asked. "What do they call it now?"

"Mormonville," Holliman asked.

"And the reason for that?" Jason asked.

"Because it's full of Mormons."

"Really?"

"Yep. Back before the war, the guy who developed this place finished it up right about the time that those Mormon fundamentalists tried to blow up the federal courthouse in Salt Lake City."

"I remember that. No one really got that those guys and regular Mormons weren't one in the same."

Holliman nodded. "Pretty much. Well, Jimmy Warrington developed it, but he was holding on by a thread. No one wanted to build here because he was a Mormon. Pretty outspoken one too.

"So, a pile of other Mormon decided to buy. Built some nice homes here too. Kept Warrington from going bankrupt until the hysteria died out."

"So, they're resistance now?" Rick asked.

Holliman nodded again. "Yeah, they've got their own persecution stories, and they're not interested in tyrants who could wipe them out with a stroke of his pen."

Jason nodded. "Can't say I blame them there."

As they reached the gate, two men in gillie suits stood up.

"Al," one of the men said with a nod.

Holliman greeted the two men by name, then turned toward Jason and Rick. "Jason and Rick Calvin, from New Eden."

The two men nodded a greeting. *Friendly bunch*, Jason thought, but said nothing. Instead, he smiled and nodded back.

Holliman led them through the iron gates and down the street. As they walked, weapons in hand, kids played in the street. Yards, once a point of pride for so many people in subdivisions like this, were now turned over toward food production. Everywhere Jason looked, vegetable plants as well as fruit bearing trees and bushes had taken the place of roses and holly.

As they got about half way around the loop, as far from the gate as they could get, a tall, lean man met them.

"Jack," Holliman said. "These are the folks I told you about."

Jack looked Rick and Jason up and down, as if sizing them up. Based on the look on the other man's face, Jason figured he wasn't particularly impressed.

"You the guy behind that half-assed attack on Somerton?"

Jason took a deep breath. "Not exactly."

"What does 'not exactly' mean?"

"It means not exactly. I wasn't calling the shots, but I probably should have done more to stop it."

Jack rolled his eyes. "Great. This is what you bring us, Al? Really?"

Holliman held up his hands defensively. "Wait a minute. You know the story about that guy down in Georgia? Went through a whole heap of guys to get his wife?"

Jack nodded.

The Somerton man nodded toward Jason.

"That's the man."

The tall man's eyebrow raised in surprise. "That so."

Jason nodded, surprised. How far had that damn story gotten? "Yeah, but I've heard it got blown out of proportion in the telling, so don't get your hopes up. Ain't like I'm looking to take out Conklin's people all by my lonesome."

The other man held out his hand. "Wouldn't dream of it. Names Jack Lassiter. Good to meet you, Mr. Calvin."

Jason took his hand. "Might as well call me Jason. I'm not big on the whole 'mister' thing."

Holliman laughed. "Only person I've ever heard call him 'Mr. Calvin' was Conklin."

He shrugged. "Bastard pissed me off."

Jack smiled. "You know, I think I like your style just fine."

** ** **

Jason wasn't sure he was still alive. I mean, he didn't remember dying, but he figured he must have died. Air conditioning sure felt an awful lot like Heaven to him.

He closed his eyes and let the cool air wash over him, a tidal wave of simple pleasure he'd thought he would never feel again.

"Nice, isn't it?" Holliman asked.

Jason nodded, his eyes still closed out of fear that opening them would take the magical coolness away.

"Most of Somerton has power. Lots of places do, really. Surprised you guys don't in New Eden."

He shrugged. "Can't say we do. Didn't have it in North Georgia either. Most of the power plants went offline after the war, didn't they?"

"Not really. Some did, but a lot of folks who worked at the plants kept them going. Manufactured parts from scratch, whatever they could. After all, their families were supported by the power too."

"The EMP?" Jason asked, remembering how the electromagnetic pulse had fried his own car, making it necessary to walk home.

"Worse in some places than others," Holliman said. "For better or worse though, there are a lot fewer customers now, so the plants that did get fragged aren't needed so much now."

Made sense to Jason. "Wonder if there's anywhere in the valley with power," he said as he opened his eyes, now mostly convinced the cool air wouldn't disappear now that he could see the world around him."

Holliman shrugged. "No clue, but worth looking into."

"Okay, so what are we doing here? I mean, as awesome as AC is again, there has to be a better reason to stop by."

Holliman nodded. "Yeah, there is. Jack is part of the resistance. A big part. These guys are better supplied than most of the folks were after the war. Most had a year or so of food, but scavenged just like everyone else, so they kept themselves better fed."

"Which, let me guess? Made them more effective at it."

Holliman nodded. "They shared what they got, but it gave them a certain standing with most folks. When Conklin came in, he took the region, but knew he couldn't hold it if he took Jack out, so he didn't."

"I take it Jack knows that's a temporary thing?"

The resistance member nodded. "That's why he's kind of a big deal with the resistance."

Lassiter walked into the room, looking somewhat amused at the sight of Jason beneath the air conditioner vent. "Am I interrupting anything?"

Jason smiled. "Just the greatest thing I've ever experienced besides my kids being born."

The other man nodded with a wry grin. "Please have a seat," he said, motioning toward a rather comfortable looking leather chair. "Can

I get you anything? Water, soda?"

"You guys have soda? I thought Mormons didn't do soft drinks?"

"Not necessarily. Coffee and tea are off limits, but soft drinks are more of a gray area. Most folks don't seem to realize it."

"Interesting." He'd studied Mormonism more than most non-Mormons, but this was new to him. Not really important either.

Jason took a seat, looking over as the other man took a seat next to him. "Jason, like I said, I like your style. However, I can't say that I trust you," Lassiter began.

"Tell me how you really feel," Jason said with a wry grin of his own.

"It's nothing personal, but your boys got their asses kicked. You wouldn't be the first people to pretend to want to attack while really just trying to get intel for Conklin to buy their way off of his list."

Jason nodded. "Fair enough. Did I mention the son of a bitch killed my wife?"

Lassiter closed his eyes for a moment, then opened them and look Jason in the eye. "I'm sorry to hear that. Unfortunately, that's not enough of a reason for me to trust you. I'm sorry for that too."

Well. This is going to shit quick, fast, and in a hurry. Despite the cool air, Jason rolled up his sleeves, digging in for a long discussion. Suddenly, he felt a hand grasp his right arm and pull. The tattoo.

"What is this?"

Crap. This doesn't sound good. Just what I need, more of this conspiracy theory shit. "Yes, I'm a Freemason. No, we're not responsible for the war."

"I know we're not."

Jason breathed a sigh of relief, then caught as he realized exactly what Lassiter said. "Wait. 'We?'"

Jack Lassiter began a series of odd, cryptic sounding questions. Jason answered equally cryptic to those who didn't know. Signs and handshakes, phrases that made little sense to most, all filling him with growing confidence.

When they'd finished, Lassiter smiled deeply. "I wanted to trust you. Needed a reason. That tattoo on your arm? Gave me what I wanted."

Jason smiled. "I'm glad, because I've got to have the help."

Lassiter nodded. "Your people."

Nodding, Jason said, "Among other things. But I can't do it alone. Officially, I'm not even here. I'm off the reservation, so to speak."

"The other man with you?"

"That's my oldest. My son. He wants some

payback for his mother."

"Seems young."

Jason nodded. "He is, but he's held his own against Conklin's boys before."

"He'll do what needs to be done?"

Jason laughed. "The biggest problem won't be him freezing up. Might just be holding him back."

** ** **

"We've got you set up. Resistance people will be waiting for you," Lassiter said as they lined up just inside the iron gate.

Jason grunted. "If we survive."

"Yeah, well, there's always that."

"So," Rick said, "it's not like we couldn't just die in our sleep or anything."

"Your son makes a valid point," Lassiter said.

Jason nodded. "You're sure they don't watch you guys?"

Lassiter nodded. "Yep. We check periodically. Random intervals. Never found anything."

Nodding, Jason said, "Alrighty then. I guess we need to get a move on."

Lassiter held out his hand. "Brother Jason. It's been a pleasure. I hope we can catch up some other time when you're not off to kill and maim my fellow Republic of Somerton citizens," he said with a smile.

Jason returned it. "I make no promises, but it would be nice."

"We ready?" Holliman interjected. Jason was surprised how antsy the other man was.

He nodded. "Yep. Let's get moving."

"Yep. Countries just don't overthrow themselves you know," Rick said, smiling. Jason raised his kid to be an optimist.

With final goodbyes made, the three men headed down the road. Rick and Jason had hidden their rifles in their packs, per Holliman's suggestion. Apparently, Conklin didn't trust his own people with guns, so carrying rifles without a uniform would have stuck out like a sore thumb. However, they were able to secure pistols beneath their clothes. They weren't idiots, after all. Luckily, the packs were big enough, and the rifles were short carbines.

"How much longer?" Jason asked. They'd been walking for hours and he had no idea where he really was.

"About a day or so. We should hit it sometime tomorrow morning," Holliman said.

Rick tugged on his pack straps, testing the tightness. "You kind of seemed in a hurry to get back. You missing out on something?"

Holliman smiled nervously. "Just be glad to be home. Even if Conklin's an ass, it's still home, you know?"

Jason nodded. "You realize you're not going to be able to take a night out on the town or anything, right?"

He nodded. "Yeah, I know. I'm really pretty cool with just hanging out with my roommate for few days."

"Out of sight?"

"Yep."

"These resistance folks of yours. How many are we looking at?"

Holliman shrugged. "Not really sure. We're mostly in a cell structure. I knew Jack and a few others from something we'd done a couple of years ago, but that's kind of unusual. We could have thousands. Might only have a dozen or so."

"Wow, Al, you're filling me with unspeakable confidence," Rick said, deadpan but still somehow dripping with sarcasm.

He laughed. "Don't get me wrong. I mean, I don't know how many, but I seriously doubt Jack would have passed the word unless he figured we could actually pull it off with the numbers there."

"So he knows?" Jason asked.

Holliman hesitated for a moment before

nodding. "Yeah. One of the few who does, but yeah."

"That means bad things for him if we get caught," Jason said.

He shrugged. "Maybe, but I don't plan on talking."

"You plan on being dead?"

Holliman stopped dead in his tracks, looking at Jason as if an appendage and sprung out of his forehead. "What the hell kind of question is that?"

Jason stopped and faced him. "It's a fair one. Look, I made a living getting people to talk to me. One of the people who talked to me was a former prisoner of war. The truth is, everyone talks eventually. You don't want to, and the longer you hold out, the more you didn't want to, but everyone talks. It's even more true if you have an asshole like Conklin who won't think of hurting other people."

He seemed to consider it for a moment, the nodded. "I guess. I'm damn sure not going to make it easy for them though."

Jason smiled. "Kind of my plan too."

Rick walked, seemingly lost in his own world. Something about his body language made Jason think that his son had no intention of going at all.

** ** **

Conklin liked it here. The dark of the basement felt more like home as he looked down on the bruised and bloody Megan Hernandez.

She was scared. He drank it in like a vampire, basking in it. Conklin knew what kind of reputation he had, a reputation for getting off on hurting women, but it was really more than that. He felt powerful.

He knew there were multiple kinds of power, and he enjoyed all of them he could get. He had the ability to have people killed with a snap of his fingers, intoxicating all on its own. He had the ability to demand things from women who didn't really want to give them, which was something else entirely. Most importantly, he enjoyed taking a stuck up bitch like this and making her scream.

"Bet you wish you'd have been nicer to me, don't you?"

Megan sobbed. For him, that was as good as any yes ever could be. The truth was, he preferred it if they weren't bitches to start with. The fun was in making them regret it.

A knock on the door drew his attention. He turned and walked to the door, opening it just a crack.

Outside, Ramirez stood. "Yeah?" he asked as he stepped through the door, closing it behind him.

"We've got a problem, sir. The OP we placed outside of that old, crazy guy's place went missing."

Conklin cursed under his breath. "Alright, meet me in my office in twenty minutes. I want everything we know about this, got it?"

Ramirez nodded. "Yes, sir."

"Good. Now get lost. I've got business to finish up down here."

The younger man nodded, spun on his heels, and walked away.

Conklin walked back into the room and closed the door, the audible *click* of the lock echoing eerily throughout the chamber.

"Now," he said as he turned and smiled wolfishly, "where were we?"

** ** **

Ramirez waited in Conklin's office. The walls filled with awards. They were all meaningless, even the ones Ramirez understood. No one cared either way, these day. No one except Conklin, anyways. Inside, he thanked God that he'd been given a bit of a reprieve from having to meet his boss immediately after seeing what he was doing to the Hernandez woman.

He considered himself a hard enough man. He'd personally killed plenty of folks and committed plenty of atrocities of his own. Somehow, though, Conklin's proclivities bothered him so much more than anything else.

To make matters worse, Ramirez knew that the woman was married. He'd pulled her and her son out of the church himself, putting the gun to the kid's head to make the husband come along quietly. He didn't have a clue why it mattered that she was married, but it did. He figured it might have had something to do with his Catholic upbringing, but that was so long ago, he didn't really know any longer. It's not like this was the only iron he had in the fire.

His reflecting ended abruptly as the office door banged open. Conklin stomped into the room, not saying a word, and plopped down on the other side of the table.

"Report," he barked.

Ramirez nodded and said, "A relief team left out several days ago on horse to the observation post outside of the old man's place. When they got there, our guys were gone. Some indication of blood, though how old it was, they couldn't tell."

Conklin said nothing for a moment. "Any

word on the OP watching New Eden?"

"Yes, sir. They radioed in via relay earlier today. They accepted relief and were returning home."

"No word on any troop movements?"

"Negative, sir. They did report that no signs of Calvin anywhere within the town, however."

"HumInt?"

"Rumor has it that he headed south to visit his mother-in-law outside of where Rome, Georgia used to be. Seems we got his wife in the shelling."

"Too bad the bastard hadn't been home at the time," Conklin muttered. In a more casual tone, he asked, "Any confirmation on that?"

"Negative, sir. None at all."

Conklin was silent once again. The silences made Ramirez nervous. He'd been there too many times when the silence meant hell on Earth was about to be brought against someone who'd done nothing wrong. Duty, however, was duty.

"Alright, there's a possibility he's coming here instead. Agreed?"

The question took Ramirez back. Conklin didn't usually ask for input unless it was in raw information. "Um...yes, sir. It's possible. If so, he's most likely only got his son with him. From what we understand, he's just a kid though."

Conklin smiled. The feral nature of that grin chilled Ramirez, though he'd had plenty of practice hiding any shivers. "He probably thinks he's being clever."

Ramirez watched as his commander stood and paced. "Oh, yeah. Finally. Someone who's seen the elephant in my presence, and still has the balls to bring the fight to me. I've been waiting for this," the man muttered. Ramirez did the best he could to interpret it, but sometimes, it was just better to ignore your boss than to accept that he was nuts.

Finally, the man stopped. "Put the city on heightened alert. If he's coming, I'd hate not to put on a spread for our guest of honor."

Ramirez had heard plenty about Jason Calvin. All indications were that the man was a true survivor. At this moment, he actually felt pity for the man.

What's coming to him is going to hurt. Better him than me though, you know?

Chapter 13

Their contact was late. They had pushed through the day, humping hard to make sure they were at the rendezvous point on time. They'd done it, actually arriving a couple of hours early.

Now, they hid in the trees on an old divided highway median. Since the war, the growth and taken over, providing plenty of concealment.

What it was wasn't comfortable.

"When the hell is this guy supposed to be here?" Rick asked with the typical patience seventeen year olds have been known for throughout the centuries.

Holliman shrugged. "Should be here."

"Yeah, I kind of noticed that," the younger man spat back.

"Easy," Jason said as he reclined against a log. "Bitching won't get them here any faster."

Rick sighed.

"Movement," Holliman whispered.

Jason moved smoothly from his reclining position to a kneeling one in a heartbeat. The other two men adjusted themselves so they could be ready for a fight in an instant.

They peered out through the dense growth. Four men in black uniforms approached.

Jason's heart pounded. Fear coursed through him, the kind of fear he hadn't experienced since the war. He battled himself as he tried to keep his breathing under control.

Minutes stretched agonizingly as they watched the soldiers approach. *Maybe they'll pass us by,* Jason thought as they got within just a few feet of their hiding spot.

"Alright," one of the men, apparently the leader, said, "We'll take it easy here for a little bit, then move back out. Water up, get something to eat."

So much for that. So, our contact is late, then these guys show up. What's next? A dragon swoops down to eat us?

Jason pulled out a folding knife he kept in his pants pocket, his palms coated with sweat. It wasn't the SOG knife he usually carried, but that was hard to carry without a sheath, and since it was integral to the gun belt, it wasn't an option. Still, it was good enough.

He glanced to the side. Rick's folder was already out and open. Holliman opened his slowly, holding the lock to eliminate the click from the black snapping into place.

Please, God, don't let me screw this one up.

Jason communicated his plans with a series

of hand gestures, mouthed words, and silent prayers. The other two nodded their understanding. He prayed silently once again.

He held up the five fingers of his left hand, his right gripping the knife. Slowly, he lowered them one by one, the delay between fingers dropping growing slight with each one.

As he lowered the last finger, he stood slowly. Two of the men had their back to the woods, but three others were in prime position. Weapons were strewn all over the ground. Jason silently thanked a benevolent God for their poor discipline.

Prayer's answered, pure dumb luck, whatever. I'm not picky. I'll take what I can get.

Jason wasn't sure how good Holliman was with a knife, but he knew it wasn't Rick's strong suit, which is why he'd picked targets the way he did.

He nodded his head, showing a confidence he didn't feel in the least.

The two men beside him bolted out of their cover, grabbed the men.

Jason had a bit farther to go, his attention focused on his targets, bursting through and making it toward the man in the center of the three remaining troops. This was the leader, and he had to be disposed of first. Years of training took over as Jason took the blade and slammed it into the man's throat, then twisted and ripped it out.

One down, Jason swung his head from side to side, looking at the two men left standing. Neither seemed interested in engaging the demon in front of them, but escape wasn't going to be an option for them.

The man to Jason's left moved first, pulling his bayonet and swinging wildly at his adversary. Jason sidestepped it easily, but almost missed the thrust from the other man.

Jason swung his blade upward and sliced the second man's wrist. Not enough to kill him, but severing the tendons and causing him to drop the bayonet.

The first man apparently saw an opening and stepped in for the kill.

He saw wrong.

Jason threw a sidekick to the man's gut, doubling him over. One opponent out of commission for the moment, Jason moved in on the second man.

His opponent was bigger than him. Bigger by a good bit actually, closer in size to Rick than Jason. Still, Jason was the one in this fight, and he was the one who had to finish it. Unfortunately for the other guy, Jason spent the last decade learning how to use a knife, spurred on by the pressure of the stories about him.

The big man swung at Jason's head. Jason ducked under the blow, the sudden move throwing him off balance. Not much, but enough that he couldn't counter.

Another punch, this time from the other side. Jason was ready.

Jason ducked again, this time shifting to the side the punch originated from. He took his blade and shoved it into the other man's armpit.

The big man screamed in pain. Jason twisted it and ripped it out.

Instinctively, the soldier threw up the other hand to protect the wound. Jason slammed the knife deep into the man's chest, right into the heart.

Jason pulled his knife out a split second before the big man collapsed, then turned toward the remaining soldier.

The other man had recovered from having the wind knocked out of him, and from the look on his face, he took that kind of personal. Jason wasn't overly worried.

"I'm gonna gut your ass," the other man said.

Jason smiled. He'd heard that before. He thought about saying something witty, but decided to channel Bruce Lee and just motion his opponent closer.

The trooper held out the bayonet

tentatively. Jason suspected this was the other man's first knife fight. He flexed his body toward the other man, who jumped back. *Yep. He's mine.*

Jason moved in. Predictably, the other man thrust toward him. Jason moved out of the way, grabbing the arm and spinning the other man until he suddenly found Jason behind him.

Jason slit the other man's throat quickly. Letting go, the body fell to the blood soaked ground.

He looked around at the carnage, his two companions finishing up their own battles.

"Well," he said, realizing he was panting for the first time when he heard his own voice, "that's a bit of a mess."

"You think?" Rick fired back.

Jason shrugged. "At least I'm not making you clean it up."

Holliman's gaze shot back and forth between the two men. "I can't tell when you're joking and when you aren't. You realize that?"

Smiling at the other man, Jason said, "Maybe it's a bit of both?"

"Shit!" Holliman said in sort of a whisper/yell hybrid. "Movement."

Jason looked. Four men headed toward them, a horse-drawn cart between two of them while the other two walked a few yards ahead.

One of the two in the lead held up his hand in greeting.

"I *really* hope that's our contact," Rick said.

Jason nodded. "You and me both, kiddo. You and me both."

** ** **

A horse-drawn cart ride might sound awesome, but Jason was having serious misgivings as the three men hung on beneath the bumping wagon. They'd secured themselves in multiple points with leather straps so they won't fall, but the ride was anything but smooth.

The cart had sides that hung down, effectively hiding them from cursory examination. Of course, if anyone looked under the wagon, they were all screwed.

Luckily, they'd apparently entered the city undetected. Around them, the once empty fields transform into the occasional building, until slowly it morphed into crowds and buildings butted up to one another.

When the wagon turned and entered a building, Jason breathed a sigh of relief. No sooner had the doors been closed and locked, he dropped to the floor.

"Well, that sucked," he announced as he took in his surroundings. He found himself inside of what looked like an old garage, the roll up door windows spray painted black long ago. The building was made of cinder blocks with at least a dozen different layers of paint, based on the pealing he saw. In the back stood a single door.

"Oh, come on, Dad. Are you the one saying you should always try new experiences?"

Jason nodded. "And now I've done that, so no need to do it again."

Rick shrugged. It was as close to a surrender he was likely to get from his son.

"Sorry about that," one of the men said, a rotund gentleman named Scott Latham. "Figured it the best way to sneak you folks into town."

Jason nodded. "Probably was. Just wasn't a lot of fun. Good thing I'm here on business, because if this was a vacation, I'd post a really nasty review on the net."

Latham put his hands on either side of his face. "Oh no! What would that do to tourist season!" he said in mock fear.

Jason smiled. He always appreciated a fellow smartass. Rick groaned. "Oh great. There's two of them."

Latham laughed. "If I can't laugh at a shitty world, what's the point in living in it?"

"So what's the plan?" Holliman asked.

"Pretty straight forward at this point. Yancey will be here in about an hour or so. He'll have the intel for you, including what assets are available, all that. Until then, it's chill out time."

Jason felt a cool blast of air as one of the contact group opened the door leading deeper into the building. "Air conditioning?"

Latham nodded.

"Okay, first thing? We meet in there."

"Jack said you guys didn't have power out your way."

Jason nodded. "Unfortunately."

The man shrugged. "I hate it for you boys. Seriously, I'd die without it. Especially after growing up in Southwest Georgia."

"Really? What part?"

"Albany," the other man answered.

"No way? Same here," Jason said.

"Jack said your name is Calvin?"

Jason nodded.

"Holy shit! I used to read your stuff in the paper all the time."

"Really?" Jason said, surprised anyone would remember his byline after all these years.

"Sure did. You're the one who broke that whole voter fraud thing, with those folks using the absentee ballots in the retirement homes."

Jason nodded. He'd been proud of that piece.

"Good stuff," Latham said. "Maybe if more people had listened to you, Albany wouldn't have become such a hellhole after the war."

"What happened?" Jason asked. Latham looked at him, apparently shocked. "We bailed right after the war. My mother-in-law has a place just north of Rome. Seemed a better place to be."

Latham shook his head, seeming to struggle with the memory. "The city commission tried to hold it together, but the gangs outnumbered the cops. It didn't take long before they took over the streets. Executed most of the commissioners just outside the civic center."

"Damn."

"Yeah, it wasn't pretty. I mean, I wasn't a big fan of most of the commission, but executed?"

Jason shook his head. "I'm still trying to figure out how the world went to hell so quickly. I mean, we got hit and hit bad, but it shouldn't have completely destroyed the country. Not unless there are nukes that hit that I don't know anything about."

Latham shrugged. "I don't think it was the war. Not by itself, anyways. It's almost like there was some invisible force at work. We lost tens of millions in the blasts, but you're right. We shouldn't have shattered like that."

"Didn't realize Albany went to hell so quickly."

"Not all of it. East Albany made it, believe it or not."

"How?" Jason asked incredulously. East Albany had always had a bad reputation that wasn't necessarily earned, but there wasn't much of a reason to believe it would fare any better than the rest of town.

"The base. The general there started grabbing every former Marine he could get, threw them in a uniform, and started securing everything he could. He even blew the bridges crossing the river. Then he started recruiting."

"How long after the war?"

Latham shook his head slightly. "Not really sure, but it was long enough that we all suspected we weren't going to hear from Uncle Sam."

"Wow. I guess I missed out on a hell of a lot."

"Yeah, but you had a family to worry about. Most of mine was in Columbus, so..."

"Sorry," Jason said. He'd seen the mushroom cloud over Columbus. He'd met up with other people who had lost people in Columbus. It never got any easier.

"Yeah, well...what can you do? You either cry about it, or deal with it. I grew up in a house where you just didn't cry about stuff. Besides, I had a daughter to worry about."

Jason nodded. He decided not to ask too many questions about the other man's personal life. No guarantee he was going to make it, and the less he knew, the better. Just in case. "Not always the worst way to deal with stuff."

Latham smiled. He looked a little like a chipmunk with his chubby cheeked filled with nuts for the winter. "Kind of what I figured."

The two men opened the door in the back and walked through it. Jason once again enjoyed the cold blast of air to an almost perverse degree. "We have so got to get AC back home."

"Help us win this, and I'll set you up myself with some cool air," Latham said.

Jason smiled. "Deal."

The time passed quickly as Jason and Rick enjoyed the simple luxury of air conditioning. The conversation seemed jovial, talking about old sports teams, movies, all the things Jason expected when a group of guys got together. It had been a long, long while.

When the door opened, Jason tensed slightly, expecting an attack. Instead, a slight man with shocking blonde hair and an angular face walked in.

"Gentlemen, gentlemen…and Scott," the new comer said with a friendly grin. He walked up to the leather sofa Jason and Rick occupied and extended a hand. "You must be our guests. I'm Yancey. Pleasure to meet you."

Jason shook his hand. "Likewise. I understand you're the man we've been waiting on?"

Yancey smiled, clearly not taking the comment as anything. "Well, I'm always inclined to be fashionably late and always love a grand entrance." His smile faded a bit, but his demeanor stayed friendly. "Seriously, I hope you guys didn't have to wait too long."

It was Jason's turn to smile. "Hey, it's comfortable in here. I'm not exactly in any rush to leave, you know?"

Yancey laughed.

Holliman, who'd been in the bathroom, stepped out and looked at Yancey. "About damn time you got here," he said, his fist clenched to the side.

"Yeah, I'm here. That a problem?" Yancey said, his bearing shifting in an instant.

Holliman cleared the distance quickly. Once again, Jason tensed up. He didn't know these guys, but had grown to like Holliman. Slowly, he balled his right hand into a fist, trying to plot where he would have to throw it while hoping it wouldn't be anything too big.

Yancey began his own march toward the

other man until the two were just a few feet apart.

Here we go.

The two men suddenly embraced one another. "About damn time you made it home," Yancey barked, his friendly smile plastered across his face once again.

"Yeah, well, got side tracked." Holliman said as the other man let go.

"So I heard."

Holliman nodded. "I take it I've been missed?"

Yancey nodded. "Yeah. It's your turn to do the dishes."

Rolling his eyes, Holliman said, "I should have figured. So damn typical. I try to end an absolute tyranny, and you're worried about whose turn it is to do what."

The new arrival shrugged. "Don't be gone for so long next time and they won't pile up on ya."

"So," Jason interjected, "I take it you two know one another?"

Holliman nodded. "Yeah, this unfortunate soul is my roommate."

"Ah. Gotcha," Jason said as he allowed himself to relax slowly. "Really didn't think this was a good time for a knockdown, drag out fight, but hey, not my party."

Yancey looked at him, allowed his smile to fade. Everything about him shifted yet again, this time from a friendly guy to a man with a mission. "Actually, I think it is your party now. We're just arranging the guest list."

** ** **

An exhausted Jason poured over the data Yancey brought yet again. He didn't have names, but he didn't need those. He had capabilities of his own forces, troop disposition of his own men, everything he needed.

Something was missing.

He looked up from the scattered pages, spread out over an old pool table. Around him, most people were asleep. A yawn snuck up on him, reminding him how little sleep he'd had lately. There would be plenty of time for sleep later.

Yancey slept soundly in an old arm chair, his feet stretched out and resting on a matching burnt orange ottoman. Jason stepped over and nudged the man's leg.

Sitting upright, Yancey stammered some incoherent mumblings before he remembered where he was. He looked up at Jason, eyes showing Jason that he was just barely awake. "Yeah?" he asked blearily.

"I need something that's not here. Think you can get it?"

Yancey rubbed his eyes with the back of his hand, trying to wipe sleep away. "Depends," he said as he yawned. "What do you need?"

"I need to know Conklin."

"No paperwork on that one." A voice shushed them, so Yancey stood up and walked toward the pool table, motioning for Jason to follow. "But I've got what we've got on it," he said, tapping his head with in index finger.

"I need to figure him out. Anything you guys have managed in the past, and how he reacted, anything."

Yancey nodded. "There's not much we've tried, to be honest. Not here. So I can't give you much there."

"Then I guess we're going to have to make some stuff up."

"Huh?"

Jason smiled at the other man. "You'll see."

Chapter 14

A hard rain fell all around him. Jason's hood was up, which helped, but that's not what the hood was for. Across from him stood the central barracks for Conklin's troops. He lurked in the shadows of an alley, watching the building.

Latham warned him that anyone he saw out was most likely either an indenture, or someone too poor to have one. There was almost no practical way to tell the difference. Whoever owned the bond was responsible for making sure the indenture did what they were supposed to do though, so he shouldn't have to worry about being questioned.

Two men stood guard outside. Yancey knew when the guard would change. The next one was 0200. Most of the men were already in for the night. The perfect time.

There.

Jason watched as two men came from inside. Both were armed, clearly the relief. The two teams spoke for a brief moment, Jason suspected they passed any relevant information. Frankly, he could give a damn.

Finally, the two men who'd been standing

outside made their way in. The newcomers settled in for their watch.

Internally, Jason counted. Occasionally, his eyes shifted to a window across the street from the barracks. However, he wasn't watching the window when the first guard dropped, a red mist spraying out the back of his head.

Okay, so how are you going to handle this one, Sport?

The second guard slammed something on the wall next to him. A siren's wail pierced through the rain as every light in the barracks clicked on.

Good to know.

Jason stepped back, going deeper into the shadows. Satisfied no one saw him, he turned and walked down the dark alley.

Down one alley, up another street, then double back through another street. Jason employed everything he could think of, but it looked like no one had seen him as he made his way to the old garage.

The door was partially up as he slipped through the crack at the bottom. As he walked into what he'd taken to calling the Team Room, the atmosphere was jovial.

"Alright folks, let's settle down."

Everyone found seats and looked at him. "Nice job, everyone. Who took the shot?" Jason asked.

All eyes shifted to Rick. The younger man seemed to demure a touch under all the attention.

"You did?" Jason asked.

Rick nodded.

"Nicely done. Now, tell me what you saw around the guards before you shot?"

The younger man seemed unsure how to answer. Jason sighed, then asked, "The button the survivor hit. Were there two of them?"

"Negative."

"You're sure?" Jason asked.

Rick nodded. "Absolutely."

Al Holliman raised his hand. "I acted as spotter. There wasn't anything. For the record, the button is just on the one wall."

"Good." Jason turned his attention to Yancey. "I've got a job for you."

Yancey looked like a deer in the headlights. "Why do I have a bad feeling about this one?"

"Have I ever steered you wrong?"

"That's a trick question, right?"

** ** **

A knock on the office door snagged Billy's attention. Simon looked back at him as he leaned in the doorway. "You wanted to see me?"

the council chairman asked.

Billy nodded. "We've got a problem. Big one."

"Let me guess. Militia."

"Yep."

"We can't create more men with dirt and good intentions. You know that."

Billy nodded once again. "Yeah, I do, but do we really need men?"

"Huh?"

"We've got men, but we don't have enough. What we need are trigger pullers, right?"

It was Simon's turn to nod.

"So, why does it have to be a man? It only takes a couple pounds of pressure to pull a trigger."

"What exactly are you talking about?"

"We train the women."

Simon opened his mouth, clearly intent on arguing. Unfortunately, the wheels in the chairman's mind were churning. He could do the math as well as Billy could. There just wasn't really any choice.

Slowly, Simon closed his mouth. "How much time?"

The big man shrugged. "No idea. Depends on what they're starting with."

He nodded. "True. Of course, plenty of them fought their way here from somewhere else. That's got to help," Simon said. "The question is, will it be enough?"

"You thinking Conklin's going to pay us another visit?"

Simon nodded. "If Jason does everything he's planning on, his primary mission is to get our people back. He's pissed, but I don't think he'd jeopardize the girls like that. So, if he gets them but doesn't take Conklin down..."

"Then we've got a whole pile of trouble headed this way."

"Exactly. And then we're screwed."

Billy shrugged. "I'm open to suggestions."

The sound of a throat clearing claimed the two men's attention. Sully stood in the hallway leading toward the stairs. "Um...well...I've got an idea."

The two men waited. It looked like Sully wasn't about to volunteer anything. "Damn it, boy. Out with it," Billy barked, a joking grin dancing at the corner of his mouth.

Sully jumped. He quickly composed himself before stepping forward.

"I know what I am, and I know what I'm not. Jason wants me to be able to hold my own in a fight, and that's just not likely to happen, but that's not because I don't respect fighters. I came here because I'd heard about Jason. Hell, the man's kind of a famous, you know?"

The two men nodded.

"Well, I didn't hear about him here. I heard about him miles away. The story of him and Jess is the first great post-war love story for God's sake."

"Is there a point?"

Sully nodded. "Yeah, there is. I know where to find people who would risk their lives for someone like Jason, even though they've never met the man."

"Where?" Simon said.

Sully proceeded to outline his plan. It wasn't a guarantee or anything, but what was? Billy and Simon agreed that this might just be the best hope for New Eden.

"Hell of an idea," Simon said quietly.

Billy nodded. "Think we can put it together in time?"

Simon shrugged. "Is there really a whole lot of choice?"

Billy shook his head. He just couldn't think of anything else.

** ** **

For three weeks, Jason lurked in the shadows of Somerton. Yancey had given him tons of intel, sure, but he needed more. Most people think of intelligence as military things.

That was part of it, sure, but he needed more than that.

The barracks were down the street, barely within sight. He didn't need to see it clearly, because that wasn't what he was focused on. No, that honor was for the cart parked just outside of the building.

Jason wiped his brow with his wrist, the glaring sun's heat bombarded all beneath it. *Probably a good thing I haven't gotten used to AC again,* he thought, trying not to smile.

He watched as the cart unloaded boards. He'd already seen these boards. He knew what they were for. What he needed to see was how things worked at this point.

The men at the cart unloading an armful of the boards, then took them inside, repeating the process several times. That was what he needed to know.

Jason turned and walked away. He'd done this a dozen times by now, and no one had seemed to spot him. A quick check over his shoulder told him that this time would be different.

Maybe he got complacent. Maybe it was just bad luck. He didn't know which. Frankly, it didn't matter. What did matter was that a young Hispanic man was following him.

It was difficult to tell, but it looked like

someone who'd been around Conklin a lot. *Ramirez? Was that it?* Jason had looked at a lot of intel, and his mind was getting a little crammed. The name sounded right though.

Jason picked up his pace. After all, he figured it could just be paranoia. As he rounded a corner, he peeked back. Ramirez had also picked up the pace.

So much for that.

Jason began running as soon as he was clear of Ramirez's line of sight. The street he found himself on was crowded with people milling about, fairly normal for a Saturday.

With each step, he wove his way through the congestion, focused on losing the tail.

A man stepped out of a shop just a few feet in front of Jason. He stopped dead, his body threatening to continue forward. The Somerton man looked him in the face, a scowl telling Jason that apparently something was his fault.

Jason nodded at the man, feigned an apologetic gesture, and continued on again.

A quick peek showed that Ramirez was still coming.

Damn.

Jason cut down another corner, sprinting hard, then cut down an alley. A quick turn back onto another street. Jason stopped for a second. *That had to do it,* he thought.

Panting, he looked back. The younger man was further back, but had somehow figured out where Jason had cut. *Son of a... That's just not right. God really hates me right now, doesn't He?*

Jason took off again, once again cutting down one road, then taking another cut. Every move he made, the younger man seemed to be right behind him.

Bastard recognizes me, and he's following me. Fifteen, twenty years younger than me too? I really hate young guys.

With every twist and turn, Jason's sense of direction became more skewed. He'd picked up how to navigate around Somerton a bit, but he wasn't a native. Ramirez was, and that was making the difference.

BANG! The gunshot rang out, echoing off the old brick buildings. A burning sensation ripped at Jason's side. He hazarded a look down. A red stain of blood was spreading on his shirt. The fact that it happened to be white wasn't likely to help him blend in.

Down there. Jason immediately took the next left down an old alley.

A pre-war dumpster sat there, butted up to a brick wall cutting the alley off from whatever was on the other side. One of the two doors sat up. Jason smiled.

** ** **

Ramirez knew the man he chased. He'd not had Conklin's up close and personal conversations, but he knew the face none the less. *So much for the bastard visiting his mother-in-law,* he thought as he ran.

He saw Calvin duck down an alley. *Gotcha, asshole,* he thought. He knew that section of alley.

Ramirez slowed down, his weapon at the ready. He'd already hit the man once, but that just made him a wounded animal. He knew all too well how dangerous that could be.

Weapon out front, he sliced the pie around the corner, swinging out wide to avoid an ambush.

There, the thought, seeing a deep red smear on the dumpster's lid. Still more blood pooled slightly just in front of the old metal box. *Got you now, you son of a bitch.*

"Ramirez to all units. Need team at the alley behind Main and Fourth," he said into his radio.

He could take Calvin himself, and probably get all the accolades Conklin could think of. None of that mattered though. What mattered was completing the mission successfully.

Around him, people stopped to gawk. "Move along," he barked, his scowl telling them it wasn't a polite suggestion.

Minutes stretched agonizingly as Ramirez waited for his back up. A glance at his watch told him they'd come quickly. He was in a foul mood anyways. Luckily, he was senior enough that he could afford it.

"We've got a potential foreign agent cornered down this way. He's dangerous as hell. I'd love to take this guy to the general, but if he looks like he's going for a weapon, we end him. Is that understood?" Ramirez said.

The team, three men who'd not been along on the trip to New Eden, nodded. They had, however, helped repulse the pathetic attack against their city. They didn't look impressed by how dangerous Calvin was. The truth be told, Ramirez wasn't sure why he figured the man was so dangerous either.

The three men held their M-4's at the ready, approaching the dumpster cautiously. Silently, Ramirez was impressed. They held no respect for New Eden, and since those were the only foreign personnel who might try to infiltrate, they knew whoever was in the dumpster was from there. Still, they approached it professionally.

Two men stood ready on the corner, one on each side, while the third man made ready to open the dumpster.

BAM!

The dumpster's metal lid slammed against the brick wall.

Each of the three men called, "Clear."

"What? What the hell do you mean, 'clear'?" Ramirez screamed, his face turning read as a murderous rage descended upon him.

"It's clear, sir."

Ramirez stormed over to the dumpster, glaring into the empty darkness. *That son of a bitch! Where the hell did he go?* Ramirez looked around. Somehow, some way, Jason Calvin had made it out of that alley without him seeing it. On one hand, he was furious. The hick had made him look like a chump in front of his own men. On the other, Ramirez figured he understood something of why the general saw this man as a worthy adversary.

"Alright, search the area. He's bleeding, so see if we can pick up a trail."

The three men acknowledge the order and went about following it. Ramirez smiled ferally. *Oh, you made it through today so far, but I know you're here now. Your ass is mine. Sooner or later, I'll get you and I'll nail your hide to the wall.*

** ** **

Jason staggered into the Team Room. It

was less because of the wound and more because he'd been chased halfway across Somerton.

"Jesus, Dad! What the hell happened?" Rick blurted, weaving his way through furniture to get to his father.

"Got made."

Yancey looked up from the papers he'd been studying. "Who?"

"I think it was Ramirez. Lost him in an alley. Climbed a dumpster and over a wall. Guess he thought I was in it."

The blonde man cursed under his breath. "That's Conklin's chief lieutenant. If he tells Conklin that he's seen you, things are going to get a lot more interesting."

Jason nodded. He'd already played out a number of scenarios as he double backed time and again, trying to make sure the trail of dripping blood wouldn't bring Conklin's goons to the garage's door. "I know. No clue how he did it either. I wasn't even close to the barracks."

"He wouldn't have to," Rick said. "He was in New Eden, right?"

Jason nodded.

"That's how. Like it or not, you're kind of memorable."

"Kid's got a point," Latham said. "Those guys who were there? They're likely to remember you. You were an official of the enemy. Chances are good, they had orders to take you out if possible during their raid."

Jason nodded. He didn't like it. Not in the least. Still, one of the most important lessons he'd ever learned was to listen to other people when they're talking sense. "We've still got some things to look at."

Rick nodded. "Yeah, and we will. In the mean time, the only thing that needs to get looked at is the extra hole you sprouted."

Sometimes, it's good to be loved. This isn't one of them, but it's the thought that counts.

Latham stepped forward, taking Jason's arm and draping it over his shoulder. "Come on, let me help get you cleaned up."

** ** **

The doctor poked and prodded Jason for what felt like an eternity. Jason had taken the worse that the doctor could dish out with the stoic nature inherent in his people. Or, if he were to put it another way, he'd say that he cried like a little baby.

The doc pronounced the wound as a clean hole all the way through, poured what felt to Jason like a gallon of alcohol into the hole, the doc sewed him up.

He sat up in bed, per doctor's orders, and looked at the men around him.

"Sorry, I'm just a hands on kind of guy."

"Bullshit," Rick said, a mischievous grin crossing his face. "You're a control freak."

"That too."

"So what's the plan?"

"Not sure yet. We need people to check where my people are at in the next few days. If they know I'm here, they're bound to adjust things a bit. I need to know how."

"More people?"

Jason nodded. "That's a definite. But I'm not sure how Conklin views me and any threat I pose. That's why I need to know how much he steps things up."

"And if he doesn't do anything?"

"He won't. He's not a complete idiot. He'll figure I'm up to something if I'm in town."

Rick nodded.

"By the way, any word from our source about Megan?"

"Yeah. She's starting to crack from what we're being told."

"See if we can get a message to her. Let her know we're here."

Rick nodded.

** ** **

"He's up to something," Conklin said. He'd heard Ramirez's report. While he'd have preferred to have taken the man already, he couldn't fault his subordinates caution. "The men who were in New Eden. They haven't reported seeing faces from there around?"

"No, sir. I checked earlier today."

Conklin nodded. "Okay. Set up our contingencies. Just in case."

"You don't consider him a threat?"

He shook his head. "It's not that. Jason Calvin is a threat. Something in his eyes, like looking into the soul of a fellow predator. Make no mistake, he's a threat. But he's alone. How much of a threat can one man be?"

Ramirez nodded. "You're not worried about the rumors of a resistance?"

He laughed. "Hardly. If it's around, they're too chicken shit to do anything. Hell, I think that shot a few weeks ago might have been Calvin."

Ramirez raised a single eyebrow in question.

"Think about it, Major. We shelled his home town, the people he swore to protect. Worse than that, we targeted his home. Maybe we got his wife apparently. Either way, he's pissed. You don't think he'd try to wage a one man harassment campaign?"

His subordinate nodded. "Absolutely, sir. However, I'd still like to operate under the assumption that he has help within the city."

Conklin bit back an angry retort and considered his subordinate's suggestion for a moment. "Do it. But don't operate on that assumption exclusively. Is that understood?"

Ramirez nodded. "Understood, sir."

"Good. Dismissed."

As Ramirez left, Conklin leaned back in his chair. Without an army, Calvin wasn't a threat to anyone. He knew that, and he saw no reason to believe Calvin didn't know that as well. Sure, a sheriff wasn't necessarily trained in warfare, but he'd seen the spark in the other man's eye.

No matter how much he tried, the Calvin's endgame eluded him. If it had been assassination, why take out a single guard, then nothing?

Conklin stood up and left the office. He needed to think, to silence the rage he felt within him. Down the hall, through the door leading to the stairs, he walked with intensity. He didn't know if there were people in the hallway or not. They were irrelevant.

His feet tapped on each step, but he felt nothing except the draw. Before he knew it, he found himself outside the door in the dusty basement. He took a deep breath, taking in the musty air. He unlocked the door and opened it.

The single bulb glowed above her as she lay on the floor. Dried blood stained the gray concrete floor.

"Get up," he barked.

Slowly, she raised her head. For weeks now, she'd refused to meet his gaze. Today was different. Her eyes locked on his, her face defiant.

He slapped her with the back of his hand, spinning her. Her back slammed against the floor.

She flipped back forward, a spring in her movement he'd not seen in some time.

"What the hell's gotten into you?"

A smile crossed her face, her eyes still locked on his. "I told you he was coming," she said.

The words sent a chill down Conklin's spine. It was an unfamiliar sensation to the man, to say the least. However, part of him actually enjoyed it.

"How do you figure anyone's coming for you?" She was right, but no need to tip his hand to her.

The smile grew. "Because he's here."

Conklin laughed mirthlessly. He felt no humor, but laughing at the bitch made the most sense to him right now. Well that and…

SLAP!

Another blow to her already battered and bruised face threw her back to the ground. "No one's here for you. You're going to be here until I get bored with you. You know that?"

She spit blood onto the floor. "You're going to get bored really soon then, asshole."

Conklin reached down, grabbing the woman by the throat. He slowly lifted her up, her limbs trying desperately to keep up with him. The defiance in her eyes slowly gave way to fear as she stood on her tip toes.

There we go. That's better. He smiled. It was the most genuine smile he'd worn in ages. He'd forgotten what being truly happy felt like.

"Even if Jason Calvin were here, do you think he'd give two shits about you? We've got some of the New Eden's women here. You're just some two-bit wetback whore."

She spit at him. The bloody saliva splashed against his cheek. He pressed the index and middle finger of his free hand against the wetness, then pulled it away so he could inspect it.

His smile faded.

Even he was surprised as he slammed the woman against the brick wall. He squeezed hard against her neck, nearly cutting off her air supply.

With his free hand, he struggled to remove his belt. Her eyes widened at the realization of what he was doing, her arms fighting with the hand grasping her neck.

"You...you think...raping me..." she choked out. Her words startled him just enough for him to loosen his grip on her throat. "Such a big man," she said, still struggling to get enough air, "you have to rape a woman to get any?"

His belt finally free, he let the woman go. He absentmindedly coiled the belt around his hand, the buckle in his palm. "Rape you? What makes you think you're worthy of me even considering raping you?"

Before she could answer, the thick leather of the belt slammed into her cheek.

Conklin smiled. *Bet that took some of the fire out of her.*

Megan Hernandez's face was away from the man. Slowly she turned until she looked into his eye.

Terry Conklin saw that he'd been mistaken. The fire wasn't gone in the least. Instead, he'd merely stoked the fire burning within the woman. If he were being honest with himself, he'd admit that the woman's fury would scare the hell out of him if she hadn't been chained.

"You know you're just getting me excited,

right?" he asked smugly.

"An impotent asshole like you? Color me unimpressed."

The bitch was mocking him. He'd been mocked enough in his life. He'd seen the looks of his fellow cadets at the Academy. They all mocked him too, though never where he could hear it. He'd worked too hard to be mocked by some Mexican whore.

The belt seemed to fly out of its own volition. Conklin couldn't remember any thought that would make it fly, though he approved the instant the leather smacked into the woman's face. Over and over again, he repeated the move. Inch by inch she shrunk into herself, trying to get away from the vicious assault.

No one would look down on him ever again.

Chapter 15

Jason sat on the couch. For weeks, he'd been busy focusing on what he needed to do. Now, due to the extra hole he'd developed, he was forced to sit.

Resting wasn't the issue. Jason intellectually understood that he needed time to heal. While the wound wasn't bad, he needed to be as strong as possible when the time came. Resting would make that happen.

The problem came about because resting also gave him time to think. Thinking brought about remembering. Remembering was the enemy. Someday, he'd soak in the memories of her. Remember every kiss, every touch, every look. Today, it was just too painful.

"Hungry?" Rick asked, holding out a sandwich.

Jason shook his head. He hadn't had an appetite for a while.

"Sleep any?" his son asked.

Again, he shook his head. He hadn't really slept much in the past few days either.

"Want to talk?"

He thought about it for a moment, then finally shook his head.

Rick sat down at the end of the couch. "I miss her too."

He looked at his son. There didn't seem to be any judgment in the younger man's face. It didn't matter. He'd judged himself enough alright.

"It's more than that."

"Oh?"

Jason knew what his son was doing. He was being goaded into talking. He'd been an expert in this kind of thing back in the day. He surprised himself when he said, "So many."

"So many what?"

"So many dead. All my fault."

Rick shrugged. "Are they?"

"Of course they are. If we'd have pulled off the raid, Conklin wouldn't have the bargaining chips he's got now. We'd have gotten our people back, and we wouldn't have lost so many of our own in the process."

Rick nodded. "Yep. Agreed on all counts. Still trying to see where that's your fault though."

"I could have-"

"Could have what?" Rick asked, interrupting him. "You didn't have command. Yeah, you might have made it work if you'd taken over. Then again, the indecision in the ranks might have killed even more."

"Don't lecture me," Jason growled. "I was there. I knew we were headed toward disaster."

"You tell McDaniel?"

Jason nodded. "Yeah, I told him. Son of a bitch didn't want to listen."

"Then suck it up, Dad. You're whining now, and you know how you feel about whiners."

"Yeah, well...it's more than just that."

Rick nodded. "Mom."

Jason reluctantly nodded. "It's been easier to keep my mind off it when I'm busy. Sitting here though?"

"About all you think about, right?"

"Pretty much. Her and Allison. At least with Allison, I can think about the future."

"It's not your fault either. You realize that, right?"

"Yeah, I know. Just can't help but feeling guilty."

"Dad, they targeted our house. Us, Simon, the rest of the council, there were more rounds that hit near our homes than anywhere else."

Jason looked up at his son, a new feeling replacing the deep depression. Rage. "What?" he asked, his voice ice cold. It wasn't the voice of a man, but the voice of death.

Rick nodded. "They were trying to kill all of us. Simon didn't tell you?"

"Not a word."

Rick shrugged. "Probably thought you knew."

Jason nodded slowly.

"Now you're pissed all over again, aren't you?"

"Yes," he said simply.

"Me too. Remember though, we can't be stupid about this, right?"

"Right."

"You're going to rest?"

Jason nodded.

"You going to do something stupid?"

He looked at his son. Rick seemed satisfied with whatever answer he found in his eyes since he simply nodded and went off, leaving the sandwich within easy reach.

No matter what happened, Jason was determined to crush Terry Conklin. Killing him was going to be too simple. He would make the other man suffer, suffer in ways beyond human imagining. Worse, Jason was going to make it a point to enjoy it.

** ** **

It had taken a couple of weeks, but the doctor finally pronounced Jason as fit. Of course, Jason was ready to go ahead with the operation regardless of what the doctor had said.

They'd checked every single thing time and again. The plan was made and in place. *If we're going to blow it, we're going to blow it right here and right now,* he thought. Being antsy didn't really help him make smooth decisions. Luckily, Rick, Al, and Yancey kept him grounded enough so that the plan seemed workable.

He looked at the watch on his arm. The second hand spun around flawlessly on the old style wind-up watch. Only a few more, then the fun would begin.

The second hand hit the twelve at the top of the watch face, but nothing happened. The watches hadn't been synchronized or anything, so he wasn't overly alarmed until another ten seconds had passed.

Jason looked back at the man behind him. As he opened his mouth, two explosions, just seconds apart, rocked the men.

He turned back to look at the barracks. Thick smoke billowed out the doors and windows of the building. The bombs placed under the stairs during the repairs seemed to have done their job just fine.

"Go," Jason ordered.

Five men, three women left from the shadow of the alley and crossed the street. Guards stood outside the door. They seemed torn, should they enter the building and try to help, or should they hold their posts. Jason didn't care.

He raised his rifle, now just a few yards away from them, the suppressor attached to the end of the weapon. *Pop. Pop. Pop.* Two rounds to the chest, one to the head. The first guard dropped.

The second guard unslung his rifle as quickly as he could, trying to shoulder it. Three more shots dropped him in his tracks.

Jason jerked his head toward the doors at the opposite end of the building. A fire team peeled off from the group and headed that way.

The entry way looked like a typical pre-war door, all glass and brushed aluminum. The glass, shattered by the explosion, littered the ground outside the barracks.

Despite the missing glass, Jason was forced to open the door due to the bar on the inside people would use to exit. The door open, he held it as the rest of his fire team entered the building.

The smoke still hung in the air, but was thin enough that Jason could see the stairs were completely wrecked. If the other stairs were in as bad a shape, at least this part of the plan was going like he'd hoped.

A member of his team pulled the door for

the first floor hallway open. No sooner than the door swung clear, a hail of bullets met them.

A young man whose name Jason couldn't remember fell as a half dozen bullets impacted him, most in the chest.

Jason ducked along the side, the cinder block walls offering a little protection. He popped around the corner, weapon up, firing a quick series of shots. Before he could see if any landed, more gunfire forced him back for cover.

"Well, if everything went too smoothly, I'd be paranoid as hell," he muttered. The woman next to him smiled.

"Bravo team, Alpha team," Jason said into his radio, a microphone hugging his throat.

"Alpha team, go ahead," the team leader called back.

"You in position?" The gunfire was chaotic, making it difficult to tell who was shooting from where.

"Affirmative."

"Peel two men off, have them hit first floor windows on the North side. I say again, North side. Kill anything that moves. Copy?"

"Copy. North side windows. Kill 'em all," the man said.

Jason looked at two of his fire team. They were on the side of the door closest to the door. "You two. You hit the South side. Same deal.

Got it?"

The two men nodded before bolting out the door. Jason swung out and fired three more shots, hitting with this second at least.

The portions of the blocks beside the door disintegrated as rifle rounds turned them into a fine gray powder. Jason ducked back, a round smacking the far wall. Based on where he'd been standing a moment before, he had no doubt it would have ruined his day.

Gunfire erupted from upstairs, the rounds splintering the wooden floor.

"Who the hell armed these assholes?" Jason asked, more to himself than anything. The woman next to him shrugged.

Another of his people popped around the corner to fire into the hallway. Rounds impacted the man's chest as he dropped his weapon and staggered back.

Jason pressed the microphone against his throat. "I've got two down. Report?"

"Bravo team. One KIA, one wounded but still combat effective," the other team leader said.

A scream from within the hallway drew Jason's attention. He peeked in, immediately drawing fire. He leaned against the wall and tried to replay the image he'd just taken in. Several of the men in the hallway lay face down on the floor, blood pooling beneath what he figured had to be rapidly cooling bodies.

Jason looked at the woman beside him. "Alright, I'm going to move to the other side. Think you can cover me?"

"Absolutely," she said confidently.

He nodded. The woman, her black hair tied in a ponytail, any figure swallowed up by the tactical gear she wore, swung around and pumped rounds into the hallway from her FAL. The thick .308 rounds tearing up the hallway as Jason sprinted to the other side of the door.

Seeing him safe on the other side, she pulled back to the relative cover of the wall.

"On three," Jason barked. The woman nodded her understanding.

He counted slowly. On three, he swung around and began firing, the suppressor completely unnecessary at this point. Jason focused on the front site, settling it on an enemy body, then squeezing the trigger like he'd been taught an eon ago by his old man. Like he'd taught Rick and he planned on teaching Allison someday.

Beside him, he heard the loud bark of the FAL as it sent its own deadly payload down range.

On the other side of the hall, he could see the other fire team making headway as well. *Soon enough,* he thought.

** ** **

Conklin pushed his plate away. Of all the indentures he'd picked up, his cook had to be the best investment so far. Oh, he had someone making sure the bitch didn't try to poison him or anything, but the woman could flat out cook.

He wiped his mouth, throwing the cloth napkin on the ornate china plate and stood and headed toward his study.

He entered the room, it's lavish Victorian-like red wallpaper with the gold design had grown on him through the years. The mahogany desk and comfortable leather chair was the reason he'd used this room long enough to let his opinion of the paper change. He settled down in the chair, opening a book. Despite the fact he was reading it, he really didn't *like* reading Dickens. However, appearances had to be made, so he studied the text.

Two loud thumps echoed through the town. His windows rattled slightly. It had been cloudy all day, the air hinting of rain coming, but this wasn't thunder. He'd been around too long to think otherwise.

Slamming the book closed, he got up and headed down the hallway.

"Simmons!" he bellowed.

"Sir," A man said, shooting upward as his commander approached.

"Send a runner. I want to know what the hell just blew up."

"Yes, sir!" the man said, saluting and running down the stairs.

Regardless of the causes, Conklin knew he wasn't going to be doing any more reading tonight, which was fine. He wasn't in the mood to listen to Dickens whine about the plight of pathetic losers like them.

He went into his bedroom. His gun belt lay across the four poster bed. He picked up the polished leather belt, the 1911 nestled snug in its holster, and put it on.

Carefully, he walked down the hall and down the stairs. When word came in, he needed to look calm and cool, but wanted to be close by to speed up his response.

Once on the first floor, he walked into the parlor. Along one wall was a bar, the one accommodation he'd insisted on having installed when he took office all those years ago. An officer was expected to entertain, after all.

He opened a bottle of what had once been twelve year old Jameson, but was now significantly older, and poured a glass. If any of his men did something like this, he knew he'd shoot them himself. However, he was the man calling the shots, so he got all the leeway he wanted.

Taking a sip of the liquor, he then walked across the room and sat down. Word would be here soon enough. He just had to look like he wasn't concerned for when that moment came.

He wasn't expecting one of his men to enter immediately with Ramirez.

"Sir," Ramirez said once he saw his commanding officer. "We're under attack."

"Where," Conklin asked, taking another sip of the whiskey.

"Barracks."

Conklin cursed under his breath. So much for a cool facade. "Alright, send the runners. Have them meet us at Rally Point Bravo," he ordered. The runner bolted, years of drilling making his response automatic.

"Calvin?" Conklin asked once the trooper was gone.

"Not sure, sir. We got some radio traffic from within the barracks, but no one there really knows who Calvin is."

"How many."

"Again, no idea sir. We've gotten conflicting reports. Less than a dozen to an entire company."

"Survivors?"

"Yes, sir. They blew the stairs between the

first and second floors. The fighting's primarily on the first."

"What does that tell you?" Conklin asked, putting on his teacher mode.

"That troop numbers are probably closer to the lower numbers supplied."

"Why do you say that?"

"A larger unit would try to enter the building and hit each floor, either coordinated or one at a time."

"Very good. I think we can safely say it's Calvin, but damned if I can figure out his endgame. Did you take your precautions?"

Ramirez nodded. "Yes, sir. I took the liberty of increasing security through the city."

Conklin nodded. Initiative could annoy him, but he tried to not let it show since it had advantages. He especially refused to let it show when it turned out the junior officer who'd shown it had been dead right.

"Very good. Let's go. I've got a man to destroy."

** ** **

The loud thumps told Rick it had begun. His father was on a different radio frequency, so he had no choice but to go by the explosions. Not that it was a problem or anything.

"Go," he said into the throat mic.

In the dark, it was difficult to see what his people were doing. They'd all taken up positions hours earlier, sneaking up on their targets. Now, he just had to wait for the results. Waiting, however, was going to be the worst part.

One by one, they called in. "Clear" each said, also giving a number which corresponded to a position. Each voice meant another guard with a quick and fatal knife wound. Once all had checked in, he said radioed the word, "Converge."

Within minutes, eight other men stood beside him. Nominally, he was in charge of this leg of the operation, though he didn't have a damn clue why. It helped that this leg of the mission had already been outlined. They just had to execute the plan.

He nodded. The men split up, groups of two going in various directions. Rick and his partner, an older man named Jordan, headed to the front door.

Two guards stood out front, weapons at port arms. It looked good, but knew it would delay either of them from actually using their weapons.

Unlike the barracks his father was hitting, there was little light outside this building. That would make aiming a little more difficult. Still, he figured that if he couldn't have precision, he'd make up for it in volume of fire.

He raised the rifle to his shoulder as he went around the corner of the building. He looked down the weapon, trying desperately to find the front site. The dark stick seemed to vanish against the black uniforms and shadows of the night.

He took a deep breath, said a silent prayer, and estimated. Slowly squeezing the trigger, the weapon responded. *Pop! Pop! Pop!* The suppressed weapon barely made a sound. An additional three rounds, making a total of six, slammed into the first guard. The man crumpled to the ground.

Rick didn't let up, continuing his fire as the resistance fighter registered what was happening and turned to engage. One lesson his father taught him seemed really applicable at this moment. "Shot until they're down," his father told him, and he did just that now. Round after round punched into the other man's body, but he had an incredible amount of will.

The guard kept trying to raise his rifle. Rick continued to fire, round after round, until his magazine went dry.

With practiced ease, he dropped the magazine, scooped another out of his tactical vest, and slammed it home. The delay for reloading was all the other man needed. The weapon was up to his shoulder.

Rick banged the release on the side of the AR, slamming the bolt home, and squeezed the trigger. In an instant, five more rounds flew down range, bringing down the guard.

When the guard hit the ground, Rick breathed a tsigh of relief. The one rule for his mission was silence. While he figured eventually men would be coming here to secure their prisoners, he didn't really see the need to invite them to the party early.

Jordan searched the guards' bodies, finally finding the keys. The man held them up, the shiny metal reflecting brilliantly in the limited light. Rick nodded, then jerked his head toward the door.

The resistance fighter nodded then sprinted toward the door.

"Clear," Rick said into his microphone as soon as the door swung open. Men fanned in from various shadows surrounding the building. As soon as all bodies entered, Rick grabbed one of the guards and drug him inside, Jordan grabbing the other.

Once inside, he closed the door and looked at his men. "Alright. Fifteen girls, varying ages, but young. We need them and quickly. Understood?"

Eight heads nodded.

"Good. Let's get to it."

They'd scattered, looking for the girls throughout the building. One by one, they brought them to Rick. As a familiar face, it made sense for him to explain the rescue.

All fifteen standing in front of him, Rick pressed on the throat mic. "All recovered."

"Copy that. ETA, five minutes," their ride's voice said over the radio.

He passed the word, mostly so the girls would know what was going on. Now, he had to settle in and wait again. Not a pleasant feeling.

** ** **

Conklin hunkered down behind a low brick wall. Rounds continued to punch into the other side. Ramirez crouched beside him.

Several of his men lay dead in the streets on the other side of the wall. Other bodies were scattered on his side of the wall, poor souls who'd tried to move for a better position and failed.

"Where are the rest of the men?" Conklin yelled, desperate to be heard over the gunfire.

"Some of our people made it out of the upper floors of the barracks. They're heading here now."

"Alright, have them circle to the west. I want to hit these sons of bitches from another direction.

Ramirez immediately began barking orders into his radio.

"Well, Major, it looks like there is a resistance movement in Somerton," Conklin conceded.

"Wish I was wrong on that, sir."

"You and me both," Conklin said. He thought for a moment. "Get some men over to the armory. We need to drop some of the building these assholes are using as sniper platforms."

Ramirez grinned. "Gladly."

Chapter 16

"That it?" Scott Latham asked his team.

"Yeah, that's all of it." Jack Ingram was a good man. Scott knew him from way back, but had been surprised to learn he was resistance as well.

"The packages?"

Jack smiled and nodded.

"Good. Get out of here and get to the rendezvous point," Scott ordered.

Scott pulled back from the building, stepping over the bodies of the guards. Men spilled out behind him, setting up wooden stands. The men then took the guards' bodies and hooked them in. Up close, it was easy to tell they were dead, but no one else was going to be allowed to get up close.

When Jason outlined his plan, this building hadn't been addressed. He was concerned about what was in here, but what else could he do.

Scott understood why. Rick Calvin told most of the resistance about his mother and what happened to her. They all felt bad about that. There'd been discussions about taking this building out before, but they'd never done it. If they had, Jess Calvin might still be alive.

Would have, should have, could have. If we'd have known and all that. I've got to stop beating myself up over this crap.

The resistance fighters loaded up on the carts and took off. Scott's part in this plan wasn't over. He could end it any time he wanted after his people were clear. His sense of the dramatic wasn't about to let that happen.

Surrounded by shadows, he settled in for a long wait. In the distance, the twin thumps told him things were starting.

He pulled out the Berretta 92 as he sat down behind a pile of trash. He still had his view of the street.

Softer pops rumbled through the air, gunfire this time. Things were well and truly underway. Jason didn't know it, but Somerton wasn't the only place having an interesting night. Throughout Terry Conklin's territory, resistance cells were acting. Finally.

For years, Scott had begged. Ever since Conklin latched onto his daughter. She'd been picked up for a petty crime, then entered indenture. He'd picked up the contract. Scott didn't have a clue what would be coming. He, the guy in charge of Somerton's safety? What could go wrong?

Scott found out. He'd never seen his daughter alive again.

He'd figured out through the years that the only thing Terry Conklin loved was power. Everything about the man screamed it. Tonight, he was losing it. Tonight, Alice would be avenged.

** ** **

Jason and his team, found themselves caught in the fatal funnel of the hallway. "How the hell did they get down here?" he muttered as he ducked behind a hasty barricade of beds and cheap furniture that surrounded their position in the center of the hallway.

Rounds smacked into the wood like raindrops on a pond during a summer storm. Flecks of wood littered both sides of the barricade.

"Sir?" one of the men asked.

"Nothing," Jason said. "Just talking to myself."

The other man nodded, his eyes wide from fear. For better or worse, Jason was afraid he had to agree. This didn't look good.

He took a deep breath and looked at his radio. He pulled it out of the pocket on his tactical vest and examined the front. Reluctantly, he changed the frequency.

"Eden One to Eden Two," he said as he

pressed the throat mic.

"Go for Eden Two," Rick's voice answered back, static distorting it slightly.

"Bad news, kiddo. We're pinned down, so it doesn't look like I'm going to get out of here."

"We're extracting the alpha packages now. Can be at your location quickly. ETA five minutes," he replied.

"Negative, Eden Two. You are to proceed on mission. Understood?"

The only response was the now lessening gunfire. *Must be pulling some of these men out to deal with one of our surprises. Too bad it isn't taking the rest of these assholes too.*

"Alright," Jason said, loud enough to be heard over the gunfire. "We're low on ammo, so conserve it right now. Take aimed shots. You squeeze the trigger, one of theirs had better drop. Got it?"

Five heads nodded.

"Alright. If we do that, we might actually survive this shit."

"All due respect," said the woman who'd stood beside him outside the hallway earlier, "I ain't holding my breath on that one."

"Probably a good call."

Jason poked his rifle through an opening in the barricade and waited. A Somerton man peeked around the opening. *Pop!* Down he went.

Another popped around. Jason fired again, the round slamming into the pockmarked wall next to the doorway. He adjusted and fired again, hitting the door jam. *Son of a bitch!* He adjusted, but the troop swung back behind the door.

When another man stepped out, he brought his weapon to bare. Before he could pull the trigger, the enemy staggered backward.

A quick look over his shoulder showed others were doing the same. *If this is it, at least we're going to die a good death.*

"Go tell the Spartans," he said an instant before firing two rounds, dropping another man. "Stranger passing by." Another squeeze of the trigger, a round through another man's left eye. "That here obedient to their laws," he said as three shots came from beside him, peppering another body. "We lie."

"If it's all the same, I'd rather they put that on my tombstone about a hundred years from now when I die of old age," the woman said.

"Kids today. No sense of the heroic," Jason said with a smile. The woman smiled back. "You prefer 'Remember the Alamo'?"

"Not particularly, but whatever floats your boat, sir."

Jason shrugged.

** ** **

Rick motioned half his team to go to the end of the building. They were still a fair ways from it, but he didn't want anyone inside to have a chance to see their approach.

He waited. Gunfire still came from inside the building. He knew that was a good sign. It didn't mean his father was still alive, but it meant there was at least a chance. Silence? Not so much.

"Alpha team, in position," the voice said over the radio.

"Copy that. Proceed." Rick looked at the rest of his team, then jerked his head toward the building. He didn't wait to see if anyone was following as he jogged across the street.

Elsewhere in town, he could hear more gunfire. Apparently one of those surprises was doing its job. He wasn't really sure what it was, exactly, not knowing the town like his father did, but he didn't really care. Things were proceeding as expected.

Rick found himself at the outside corner of the building, the bodies of the guards still laying on the low steps leading to the door. He pressed the mic and said, "Go."

He stepped into the opening, his target backlit beautifully for him. He senses his people moving into position.

The enemy's focus was down the hall. They hadn't seen them. A smile curled his lips. *Lambs to the slaughter.*

Rick squeezed his trigger, rounds spinning down the barrel and out into the brightly lit stairway and slamming into the unsuspecting Somerton soldier. Around him, the roar of gunfire engulfed his entire world like a warm blanket, making him feel bizarrely safe.

In just seconds, Ricks end of the hallway was devoid of human life. He opened the door and ushered his team in.

Silence came from the other end of the hallway as well. They'd succeeded as well.

Rick pulled out a small mirror, meant to signal help in the case of an emergency, and looked down the hall. No heads popped up. Either they were all dead, which was unlikely, or...

"Hold your fire!" Rick yelled.

Silence met him for a few moments, then a tentative voice said, "Rick?"

"Yep," he answered. His father's voice quashing any lingering anxiety. Rick stepped into the doorway.

"Didn't I tell you to proceed on mission?" Jason said, standing up from behind a ragged pile of wood and mattress.

"I haven't done what you told me for seventeen years. What made you think I'd start now?"

Jason seemed to consider it for a moment. "Fair enough."

"We need to get the hell out of here though. I don't know if these guys had a chance to call for help, but I'd rather not find out that relief is on the way, you know?"

Jason nodded. "Agreed. Everyone else?"

Rick shrugged. "We sent the second group to escort the wagon and headed this way."

"Alright. Let's get the hell out of here."

Every fiber in Rick's being agreed with that assessment. There was still a long way to go.

** ** **

These bastards are going to be sorry for trying to embarrass me in my own city, Conklin thought as he walked in front of the column of soldiers. He'd managed to get away from the kill zone, Ramirez beside him.

Now, he and what men he could gather headed toward to the one place that would make the bastards pay. He'd level the damned area if he had to. Sure, the business owners would bitch, but he could deal with that. Anyone who couldn't learn to shut the hell up, well, that's why guns were invented.

Outside the armory, the guards still stood their post. He'd trained these men well. They didn't abandon their posts, even to help their brethren.

For some odd reason, he noticed the two men didn't even bother to look their way. A large formation of men marching toward the armory in the middle of the night should have at least elicited a look. That is, unless...

Conklin turned toward Ramirez. "It's a tra-"

His voice was cut off by the thundering explosion. Before his mind could even register what was happening, the pressure wave from the massive blast picked him up and threw him back. Out one corner of his eye, he saw Ramirez doing the same.

Gravity slammed him back to the Earth abruptly, knocking the wind out of him. While still conscious, he hurt everywhere. A pounding headache felt like a metal spike had been driven through his skull.

"Sir," Ramirez said, his voice sounding distant. Conklin noticed a ringing in his ears. "Are you alright?" the younger man asked.

"Yeah," he answered. "I'm fine. The men?" He held out his hand.

Ramirez took the hand and helped his commander to his feet. "Nothing major. Mostly battered and bruised."

Conklin nodded. "Set up a perimeter. Have the runners pass the word that this is the new rally point."

"Here, sir?"

He nodded. "Are we being shot at, Major?"

"Negative, sir."

"Then here is good enough. Post men to keep our people out of that kill box that *used* to be our rally point."

"Yes, sir." Ramirez turned and began grabbing men and issuing orders.

He couldn't tell his subordinate. He hated the idea of using this as a rally point, but he was out of options. Some two-bit small town sheriff had bested him so far. Attempts to communicate with the men watching the prisoners had failed. Those girls were gone. Now, the best weapons he had to exact revenge were gone as well now that the armory had blown. Zulu Company still had some tubes, but the rounds were stored in the armory. All of those were gone as best he could tell.

I swear to God, I'm going to destroy everything that rat bastard loves. That town? I'm not going to leave anything but a smoking crater…wait, I can't, because the son of a bitch blew up my ordinance. Fucker!

He needed to think. If Calvin was in charge of this, then maybe he could figure something out. Everyone had tendencies. They had patterns. Once you knew them, you owned them. Now, he just had to settle down and think. Calvin had already showed his tendencies. Conklin just had to think about them for a moment, and all would be revealed.

** ** **

Scott Latham walked carefully, keeping to the shadows. He had another stop to make, but he had to make sure Conklin knew what had happened. Did it offer risks? Sure. But it was worth it in his mind.

Yancey stood outside of the large Victorian home, an enclosed cart with its horse and a driver pulled up nearby. Scott looked around to make sure the coast was clear, then stepped out of the shadow for the first time since settling in to wait for Conklin.

"How's stuff?" Yancey asked.

"Wonderful. You?"

Yancey smiled. "Sounds like about the same for me." He jerked his head toward the door.

Scott nodded and followed the other man up the steps. Yancey knocked on the door.

A few moments later, the distinctive click of a lock being opened told them the door would open momentarily.

The door creaked open, just a few inches. A chain apparently still kept the door secure. A wrinkled female face appeared in the crack. "Yes? Can I help you?"

Yancey stepped forward. "Hi there. I spoke with Stephen earlier about purchasing the contract on a couple of indentures?"

"Oh yes, Stevie said you might be coming by." The door closed. A rattle indicated the woman was removing the chain.

The door reopened. "Please, please, come on in. Can I get you anything?"

Yancey smiled, his charm oozing. "No, thank you, ma'am. We still have a lot to do tonight. Plus it sounds like we might get some rain."

"I *thought* I heard some thunder earlier. Stevie's so paranoid though. He's convinced something blew up," she said with a laugh.

"Is Stephen still here?"

"No, no, he's out. Said he had some Army business."

"Really? Well, did he happen to tell you about our discussion?"

The old lady nodded. "Oh yes. He said you were going to deed him fifteen bushels for each?"

Yancey nodded. "Absolutely. Quite a bargain if you ask me."

She sighed. "You might think that, but these two? They're runners."

"I know. Stephen told me. That's alright though. Where they're going to be, they won't be running away from," he said with a disarming smile.

"Good. Thieves. That's what they did, you know. Then they ran. Another one ran too, but Mr. Conklin has her all safe and sound."

Yancey nodded. "Absolutely, and that will probably discourage these two from trying to run."

The old woman shrugged. "Maybe. You know how *they* are. Probably don't look at loyalty the same way folks like us do."

Scott fought the urge to laugh. *If only you knew.*

Yancey nodded sagely. "I'm quite sure you're right." He reached into his vest, pulling out a piece of paper. "Here's the deed Stephen and I agreed upon."

The woman opened the paper and examined it carefully. Eventually, she nodded and folded it back up. "Come with me. I'd bring them to you, but at my age…"

"Oh, that's quite alright. We don't mind at all. That's why I brought my man with me," Yancey said, gesturing toward Scott.

The woman nodded, then turned and walked down the hall. The two men followed her down the stairs into an old basement. As Scott looked around, he saw the narrow windows had been barred, effectively turning the basement into a prison.

Two males sat hunched into one corner of the empty basement. One much older than the other, apparently the father.

"There they are," the woman said, handing Yancey a set of keys.

He smiled at the woman. "Thank you, so very much." He turned his attention toward the two. The smile vanished. "Get your sorry asses up!"

The two indentures stood up slowly. Their hands shackled to the floor, there was only so much standing the older of the two could actually do.

"I'm going to unchain you from the floor. If you even think of moving wrong, my man here will beat you into a bloody paste. Is that understood?"

Timid nods answered him.

"Good." Yancey bent over and unlocked the lock keeping their chains to the floor. He took the chain in his hand and began walking back toward the woman, using the chain as a leash.

"Here you are, ma'am," Yancey told the old woman, offering her the key back.

She smiled, taking the key with on hand and offering a different key with the other. "This'll be for their wrists."

"Thank you so much. It's been an absolute delight to meet you this evening," Yancey said.

The older woman smiled, the look on her face saying she wished she'd been about forty years younger.

They made their way upstairs and out the door, wishing the old lady a wonderful evening. Yancey drug the two indentures up into the enclosed cart, Scott closing the door behind them.

"Thank God that's over," Yancey said, his pleasant smile back. "Please accept my apologies for my behavior in there. We had to sell it, you know."

The older man looked around the interior, clearly confused. "Sell it?"

Scott sat down on one of the benches running along either side of the cart. As Yancey unlocked the shackles on the wrist, Scott gestured toward the bench.

"Mr. Hernandez, my name is Scott Latham. We're here at get you at the request of Jason Calvin."

At the mention of Calvin's name, the man's

eyes widened in surprise. "You mean...?"

Scott nodded with a smile.

"Megan?" he asked, terror gripping his voice.

"We're going to get her next," Yancey offered as he banged on the wall between the cabin inside and the driver.

Hernandez hugged his son, now also freshly unshackled. The two of them crying quietly.

The trip from the house to Conklin's headquarters building was short. Outside stood a man in Somerton black. Luckily, Yancey knew the man, greeting him as soon as they got out of the wagon.

"This way," the man said. Yancey failed to introduce him, and Scott didn't bother to ask.

The new man lead them down into a dank, dusty basement. The basement had been divided into multiple rooms, but only one had a closed door. The new man pulled out a ring of keys and unlocked the door.

Scott intellectually knew what he would see. He knew what his own daughter had looked like in her casket. None of that really prepared him for what he was seeing.

Megan Hernandez was supposed to be a very attractive woman. She might have been. She might be again someday in the future. Right now, all Scott could see was what could best be described as a living, breathing bruise.

Her nose sat crooked on her face, her eyes swollen so badly, he wasn't even sure she could see.

Scott walked forward as their guide began unlocking the woman's chains. "Megan Hernandez?"

The woman nodded.

"My name is Scott. I believe you're expecting us? We're here with Jason."

She muttered something. Try as he did, he couldn't hear it. "I'm sorry?" he asked, moving closer in hopes of making out her weak words.

"What kept you?" she whispered.

That took Scott aback a bit. He looked at the woman, her wounded and battered face. The corners of her mouth curled up in a smile.

"You're the one who let her know we were coming?" Scott asked the stranger.

He nodded. "Yeah. Snuck in when I dropped off her food to let her know."

"Thanks," Scott said, pulling up one of the woman's arms and wrapping it over his shoulder. Yancey did similar. Slowly, they lifted her off the floor, her feet dragging behind her as they took her to be reunited with her family.

Chapter 17

The rally point they'd chosen was the same place Jason had used during the failed raid. Wisdom said it was a bad idea, because no doubt Conklin knew they'd used this point and would look here again. Unfortunately, Jason didn't have time to find a better spot.

He, Rick, and their surviving teams had gotten here shortly after the New Eden women had. Waiting for them had been a couple hundred resistance fighters.

Al Holliman stepped forward, shaking their hands. "This is your escort."

Jason smiled. "Wish we didn't need one."

Holliman nodded. "Yeah, me too. Of course, I don't expect Conklin to take this particularly well."

"You think?" Rick popped off. "They'll be after us as soon as they can. Think your boys in town can keep their heads down long enough to get us a head start?"

"Not sure. They're going to try, but this is just the start for us. We can't sacrifice people right now without a damn good reason. No offense, but..."

"What do you mean, 'just the start'?" Jason

asked.

Holliman took a deep breath. "Well, we figured this was a good time to really stir crap up, so resistance units throughout Somerton's territory rose up tonight. We're fighting in almost every town."

"Why didn't someone say anything?"

"Honestly? We weren't sure if you'd feel like you'd been used or something. You were beating yourself up pretty bad for a while there."

Jason thought about it for a moment, ready to protest, but stopped himself. The other man was right, after all. He'd been beating himself up for everything that had happened. "Well, for what it's worth, it's actually a relief."

Holliman seemed surprised. "Oh?"

"Yeah. It means relief won't be coming from outside of town if they're all tied up with uprisings in their own area of operations, right?"

Holliman seemed to consider it for a moment. "Yeah, I guess so. Didn't really think about it that way."

Jason shrugged. "No big."

As more people trickled in, everyone who'd been in the fight restocked their ammo or replaced missing gear from a cart that had come from the town's armory. Tons of 5.56 rounds, plenty of 9mm, everything they needed.

The two wagons were finally joined by an

enclosed cart. The cart bounced up and down on the rough ground before coming to a stop. A door mounted in the back swung open, letting Scott Latham and Yancey step out. "Gentlemen! We have arrived," Yancey boasted, his arms held out in victory.

Despite himself, Jason smiled. Yancey had missed out on the fighting, but here he was.

Following the two resistance members was Mark Hernandez. The man looked pissed. Jason couldn't say he blamed them man. He'd heard what Megan was going through. Jason knew what he'd do to anyone who'd done that to Jess. Hell, he'd done horrible things to a man who'd simply kidnapped her. Her ordeal was a cakewalk compared to what Megan had endured.

Mark walked up to Jason and, without saying a word, punched him right in the jaw.

"You son of a bitch! Where were you? You could get us out, but not before that son of a bitch hurt her. You could have left me, but why didn't you come and save my wife sooner?"

Jason felt an icy rage flowing over him. He took a deep breath, trying desperately to keep it in check. Every ounce of intellect told him that Mark Hernandez didn't have any idea what had happened.

"I'm sorry I couldn't save your wife sooner.

I was burying mine," he said, the icy tone meant as a warning to the other man.

Mark Hernandez look like he'd been punched far harder, even staggering back a step. "Oh God. I'm...I'm so sorry. I...I didn't know."

The rage mostly gone, Jason nodded. "I know," he said. The rational part of his mind was slowly taking back control.

"Plus, just so you know," Rick said, "he got shot while trying to plan out how to spring you guys. You might want to try a little gratitude next time. Just sayin'."

Mark eyed the younger man, his own rage seeming to war with rationality. Finally, he nodded. "You're right. Thank you. Thank all you folks," he said, the last bit loud enough for everyone to hear it.

Jason nodded. "We're still not out of this."

Mark looked back at him, confused look on his face.

"Conklin doesn't seem like the type to just decide to let bygones be bygones," Rick said.

The newly freed man's eyes widened for a moment, fear clear for everyone to see, but just for a moment. Any terror he showed soon vanished, an icy resolve taking its place. "What can I do?"

"You know how to shoot?" Rick asked.

Mark shook his head. The answer surprised

Jason. He'd seen so much fighting that he just couldn't imagine other people hadn't.

"No," Mark said. "But there's got to be something I can do."

Rick nodded. "Yeah, there is. Think you feel up to running ammo?"

The other man nodded.

"Good. Head on over to the ammo wagon and load up." Rick smiled at him as he turned to walk away.

"Doesn't know how to shoot?" Jason muttered.

Rick chuckled. "Not everyone's a gunslinger, Dad. You talk about the switch everyone has in them, but you seem to miss that most people just don't want to get into it."

"Yeah, but…I mean, how did they make it?"

Rich shrugged. "From what you've told me, most every fight you got into was because you wouldn't sacrifice your principles or your life. Most folks? They'd rather not, but more than that they wanted to just get by."

"How in the hell…" Jason said, confused.

Rick patted his father on the shoulder. "You assumed everyone was like you. But, you know, this isn't really the time for all that."

Jason shook his head, trying to knock the rampaging questions out. "Yeah, I know."

Scott Latham appeared, seemingly out of nowhere, beside Jason. "I've got one of my men stashed. He's got a radio and a Remington 700."

"Sniper?" Jason asked.

Latham nodded.

"Good. He'll give us some warning if nothing else. Is everyone here?"

"Yeah. Everyone who's coming is here."

"Alright, here's the plan," Jason said. "The wagon with the girls keeps pushing through. We switch horses if we have to with the ammo wagon, but stops will be minimal. Maybe even through the night if we have to. Rick?"

The younger man nodded.

"You're going with a few men for escort duty."

"You're not keeping me out of this-"

"I'm not trying to," Jason interrupted. "It's not like we've had a chance to let the folks at home know what the hell is going on. I want them seeing you first, so they know we're not a threat."

Rick took a deep breath, eventually nodding his understanding.

"Okay, everyone else? If you're not on escort, we're going to make Conklin pay for every single mile. We're going to engage, make them bleed, then pull back a few miles. Understood?" He looked around heads nodding.

"I've got a handful of guys who brought horses. They might be your best bet as escorts," Latham said.

Jason nodded. "Good. Get them with Rick, and get them the hell out of here."

Latham nodded and headed off. Jason headed toward the man driving the wagon. They had a few things to work out.

** ** **

The woods were quiet. Birds quit chirping some time back. Even the squirrels seemed to sense something dark was coming. *Smart little bastards*, Jason thought.

"I've got them. Looks like three hundred yards," Latham's sniper said over the radio.

"Understood. You're weapons free," Jason replied.

The loud report of a .308 rifle echoed through the trees. Jason looked around. Every tree had someone behind it. He didn't really like the position, but there hadn't been time to make anything better.

Another gunshot sounded. *"Two down. Relocating,"* the sniper said.

He rubbed his palms, sweat forming under the early morning sun already. It was going to be hot. *Just once, can I risk my life on a beautiful, comfortable day?*

The silence stretched on. The sniper should have been in position by now, but nothing happened. "Status," Jason called.

"Repositioned. Standing by to acquire target."

"Understood. You're clear to engage once target has been reacquired."

Jason settled in and waited. What felt like an eternity later, two loud gunshots sounded in the distance, followed by a thundering boom. He waited for the response from the sniper.

Nothing.

"Status?" he asked.

Still nothing.

"Status?" he asked again, urgency seeping into his voice.

Still nothing.

Latham crouched behind a tree close to him. "Well, sounds like I've got bad news for ya."

Latham nodded. "I heard."

Jason keyed the mic. "Foxtrot Charlie." He switched the frequency on his radio. Around him, others made the switch as well.

He took a deep breath. "I wish your boy could have given us a count at the least."

Latham nodded.

Jason's heart began beating faster, harder,

as if it were trying to burst out of his chest. *Settle down. It's not like we're going to make it out of this alive anyways,* he thought. *Then again, that's probably not the best thought to have when you're trying not to freak the hell out.*

Moments stretched into minutes. Minutes stretched into an hour. Still no signs of Conklin's men.

Latham whispered, "Maybe they all went home for ice cream?"

Jason smiled. "Least then could have asked if we wanted any."

A flash of black in the distance caught his attention. "Never mind," Jason whispered. "They're sticking around for a bit longer."

Latham looked at him quizzically. Jason motioned toward his eyes, then pointed in the direction. Again, black stood out against the forest around it.

"Alright folks, it looks like it's almost party time. Keep an eye out. They're trying to be sneaky," he said into the throat mic.

More and more of Somerton's troops appeared in the distance. They were good though. Jason knew that black, contrary to what a lot of people think, actually stands out in most environments. The woods, for example.

Close enough.

He looked down the AR-15 in his hands.

He'd taken off the suppressor. Silence had its place, but the plan called for him to actually make a little noise.

A Somerton soldier stood next to a tree. Jason settled the front site on the man and waited a moment. "Stand by," he ordered, the prearranged command to get ready. He focused on his breathing, trying to get the chest pounding under control. The target was about a hundred yards away. Not an overly difficult shot, but not exactly close range either. The pounding slowly subsided.

Jason carefully squeezed the trigger. His round tore through the air, the shockwave of its passage sending a loud *crack* through the air. Soon, the woods were filled with a chorus of rounds, each obliterating the sound barrier as they tore into unsuspecting Somerton soldiers.

** ** **

A chorus of gunshots tore into the men around Conklin. "Return fire!" he ordered, bringing his own rifle up and squeezing round after round down range.

The men who survived the initial onslaught followed his lead. The air between the two groups became copper jacketed hell, a landscape in which no living thing would dare attempt to traverse.

Each pull of the trigger fueled Conklin's rage. That was because he knew each round was wasted unless it hit Jason Calvin in the heart. Or the face. He'd have been pretty happy with that as well.

"Sir," Ramirez said. He practically yelled, trying to be heard over the shooting.

"What?" he asked, annoyed at the question.

"We need you to pull back."

"No way in hell. I'm going to kill that son of a bitch!"

Ramirez stepped in front of him, forcing him to hold his fire. "Sir, they've had at least one sniper. There may be others, and you're standing out here like a big target."

Conklin felt the trigger beneath his index finger. Just a few pound of pressure, and the insolence would end. No one could tell him what to do.

What the hell are you doing. Pull it together, he thought, releasing the trigger. Slowly, he nodded. "You're right. Yeah, you're right."

Ramirez motioned to two men who stood on either side of Conklin, weapons at the ready.

"Um…Keep putting pressure on their middle. If that doesn't push them back soon, we're going to pull around and hit them on the flank." Conklin felt like was in some kind of haze, almost like he were drunk.

"Yes, sir. We're on it," the younger man said, not softly, but with as much tenderness as possible considering the volume he was forced to speak at.

Conklin staggered away from the line. He didn't know what was wrong, but it was pissing him off.

He shook his head, trying to clear it. Slowly, his focus returned. He took a deep breath in, holding it for a few seconds before exhaling.

"Alright, you two. I'm good. Get back in there. Get me a count on the enemy."

"Yes, sir," one of the men said before turning and heading back toward the front. He wasn't sure what the hell had happened, but he couldn't allow it to happen again. Weakness was not to be tolerated. He didn't tolerate it from anyone, and definitely not himself.

Don't worry, Calvin. I'll get to you soon enough. You, that shitball town you call home, all of it. You stepped in it and I'm going to enjoy making you suffer.

People like Calvin had always pissed him off. He knew nothing about the other man's background, yet he knew everything. Smart, probably one of those people who had everything growing up. Conklin hated pricks like that.

He examined his lines, his men. *His* men.

289

These men were loyal to Conklin. They didn't care about how little he had growing up. They were real men. Not pricks like Calvin. Oh, he knew Calvin laughed at him, probably knew what he'd grown up with and mocked him because of it.

No, *his* men would never do that. Utterly loyal. Victory always made men loyal. He was determined to give them another one. He'd destroy his nemesis, then indenture everyone left in that town.

The thought gave him a smile. The next few days were going to be long, but what would come next would be worth the wait.

** ** **

"We're going to have to pull back," Jason yelled.

"Ya think?" Latham asked as he changed a magazine.

"Well, if we kill all of them, the other teams are going to get kind of pissed, you know?"

"Oh, well, we wouldn't want that, now would we," Latham said before rolling his eyes.

Mark Hernandez ducked down behind Jason. Around the three men, splinters rained down as enemy fire reduced the mighty pine trees into toothpicks. "Need any?" he asked, holding out magazines.

Jason grabbed a handful and stuffed them into pouches on his tactical vest. Mark threw some to Latham one at a time. The man snatched them deftly out of the air and stuffed them into his own vest.

"Mark," Jason said, "I need you to pass the word for everyone to get ready to haul ass."

Hernandez nodded, then took off down the line.

"Think he'll survive to tell anyone?" Latham asked.

Jason shrugged. "I'm not completely sure I'm going to survive to give the damn order." He brought the rifle up and fired. The round slammed into the chest of a Somerton soldier.

His men were slowing down, conserving ammo. Mark was running as much as he could, but he couldn't be everywhere.

Meanwhile, Conklin seemed to have half of Somerton out there with him. He'd estimated at least a thousand, if not two. He'd broken his men into three teams, about a hundred each. *Twenty to one odds make for awesome stories, but in real life? Yeah, they suck.*

Another Somerton man showed his face, but that was all. Jason's earlier anxiety was gone. He settled the front site on the man, right between the eyes. He carefully squeezed the trigger. The AR bucked against him as the round zipped across the hundred or so yards. The man dropped out of sight. For several minutes, he took aim and fired. He couldn't help but remember footage from Vietnam his father made him watch. One man in a trench held up his M-16 and unleashed with it, fully automatic, not even looking at the enemy. *The joys of unlimited supplies,* Jason thought.

Kind of wish I could do that too, now that I think about it.

Finally, Jason was sure everyone would be ready. He pressed against the throat mic and said, "Team one, Ohio. I say again, Ohio."

At the top of his lungs, he yelled, "Ohio!" since not everyone had a radio. Up and down the line, he heard other men call out the same thing.

Their rate of fire intensified as men began a fighting retreat. Enemy fire slacked off as the men pulled back.

Soon they found themselves jogging through the woods, sporadic gunfire behind them as the harassers did their jobs. For several miles, they moved as quickly as they could until they made it to the road. From here, the road wasn't the most direct route to New Eden, but it was the most level and therefore the fastest way there.

"Thunder!" a voice challenged.

"Flash," someone responded.

Heads popped up from the brush to either side of the road. Al Holliman jogged up to Jason. "We're in good position here. How far are they?"

"Not sure. We've got some skirmishers trying to make them think twice about coming on, so it might be a little while."

Holliman nodded and smiled. "We'll be ready for them."

"Good. There's at least a thousand, probably more. Make them bleed, but don't get stupid about it."

"We won't."

As Jason and his people pushed on, they ran into Yancey's team. The friendly man had apparently been an officer in Conklin's military at one point, and knew most of these men from there. It made sense to put him in charge. There's been no word from the skirmishers, but that wasn't particularly surprising. Their orders had been to peel off and make it to this direction as best they could. At least they knew the challenges and responses.

A few more miles, they found a spot at the base of two mountains. Jason quickly surveyed the area and declared this the perfect spot. Latham took half the men onto one of the mountain slopes, Jason taking the other half to the other slope.

The next several hours involved building fighting positions. It wouldn't necessarily stop the rounds, but it would hide them and make it difficult to figure out where to aim. Anything that could give them an edge would be welcomed.

Jason and Scott both had been careful of where to place their positions. There had to be enough ground cover that their positions would not only look natural, but that the growth would also conceal their withdrawal.

Latham moved over the road, meeting Jason in the middle. "Got something for ya."

"What's that?"

Latham smiled. "My mad bomber?"

"Yeah?" Jason asked cautiously.

"He's got some surprises he wants to set for our friend."

"There's more of that dynamite?"

Latham nodded.

"And he carried that old, nasty stuff with him?"

Latham nodded again.

"Why isn't he dead?"

"He says dying would make his in-laws way to happy."

"Fair enough. What's he got in mind?"

"About a mile down the road, set a trip wire after the last of the teams makes it by."

Jason thought about it for a moment, but his gut reaction never changed. "Tell him to do it, but as soon as it's set, he's to get his ass back here. Copy?"

Latham nodded. "He's also got something else in mind."

"Do I really want to know?"

He shrugged. "Maybe, maybe not. But I think it's a hell of an idea."

"What?"

Latham outlined what the resident explosives expert wanted to do with his old dynamite. Considering how volatile that stuff could be, he tended to want to support anything that would mean they weren't carrying it over bumpy mountain roads.

On the other hand, what Latham was suggesting could be risky for them. Still, if it was done right... "Alright, get it done. Just make sure everyone knows what the hell is going on. We don't need anyone starting the party early."

Latham nodded, then turned and headed back.

Jason went back to his position and settled in. Team leaders set up a watch schedule. The three day trip to New Eden might take longer, but so be it. If they were lucky, Conklin would get tired of this crap and go home.

He wasn't holding his breath.

The minutes ticked by, the sun making its way across the sky. Hours had passed when he got word the skirmishers had made it back. Most of them, anyways. Of the ten men chosen, eight made it back.

Another couple of hours, most of which Jason spent asleep, Holliman's group came by. They'd been challenged, but responded.

Jason went down the hill to meet up with the other leader. "Get a good count?" he asked.

"More like fifteen hundred, but we figure it was closer to two when you made contact. I'm not sure how many there now, but Yancey'll give you a count when he come by."

"Good. Head on out, get set up, get some rest, all that."

Holliman nodded.

More time passed. Men were getting antsy, waiting having a worse impact on them than the actual fighting. When Yancey's team passed, it was almost a relief. At least something would be happening soon.

No one slept now. No one talked. No one did anything more than breath until the boom rattled throughout the mountains. Jason smiled. All he thought about was Jess.

Still more waiting. Jason's stomach felt like

it was prom night all over again. Nervous anticipation rather than the near crippling anxiety from earlier.

The narrow valley the road ran through gave him a good view, good enough to see Conklin's men moving forward. Cautiously.

Slowly, the enemy moved down the road. Conklin had flankers out, trying to spook them into acting too soon. "Don't jump. That's what they're trying to force, so don't make the son of a bitch's day," he whispered into the mic.

With each tentative step Conklin's men made, Jason's nervousness grew. He tried to will it away, only to feel it continue to grow.

Finally, everything was ready. Jason aimed and fired, dropping a Somerton man in his tracks.

Like before, the world erupted into chaos as the round flew with deadly precision. Conklin's men returned fire in an instant, now warier than they had been in the first fight.

Fire came fast and heavy from the numerically superior force. Their barricade was being chewed to pieces. Jason cursed under his breath. "Idaho. I say again, Idaho."

He didn't like pulling back this quickly, but he couldn't afford to keep dealing with this rate of fire. They were ready this time. "Idaho," he yelled, his called echoed down the line.

As the pulled back, he took a quick look. From what he could tell, they'd bled him just a bit more. Not as much as he'd have liked, but he'd take what he could get.

Chapter 18

For three days, Rick has pushed them. Hard. As the houses of New Eden came into view, he finally allowed himself to breathe a sigh of relief.

Billy stood outside of town, a battered AK in his hands.

"Hold up here. Let me go talk to him," Rick said.

Stewart, the driver, nodded.

Rick walked up to his father's friend. "Fifteen New Eden residents wanting to see their families," he said.

The big man smiled. "Good to see you back. Your dad?"

"He's out there, putting a hurt on the son of a bitch. At least, that's what he's trying to do."

The deputy nodded. "Know which way they're coming?"

Rick nodded. "Too bad we don't have a militia anymore."

Billy smiled. "Well..." He outlined to Rick what all had happened since they'd been gone. The young man smiled. There was no joy in it, only feral anticipation.

"How long to get ready?"

"It's ready now. Get fed, cleaned up, for God's sake see your sister, and we can head out."

"Will do."

** ** **

Four days of fighting were taking their toll. Jason's feet drug the ground with each step. They were all exhausted.

The three teams were now down to two. Yancey had been shot and taken on to New Eden for medical care. Jason didn't know how much longer they could hold out.

Jason collapsed next to a fallen tree. "I don't know how much more we've got," he said.

Latham and Holliman nodded. Conklin wasn't some incompetent. No, he was good. His men adjusted to changing tactics quickly. They'd already lost a third of their number. While Conklin might have lost a similar percentage, he had a lot more to start with.

"You pushing back?"

Jason took a look around. "No. We can't. We're five miles or so from New Eden."

"Eden Two to Eden One," the radio squawked, Rick's voice calling him.

Jason's eyes widened in surprise. The other

two men exchanged looks with one another.

"Eden One. Go ahead,"

"What's your status?"

"Tired as hell," he answered frankly. So far, there hadn't been any indication that Conklin's men were listening to their radio traffic, and Jason was just too tired to try to disassemble.

"Understood. Our paranoid friend has you on camera. We're bringing some help, but it'll be a little while." So Milton was watching them. Made sense. They weren't that far from his place.

"How long?"

"A few hours. Your pursuit is about an hour away from you at current pace, so you'll need to hold for about two. Can you hold?"

Jason nodded, then caught himself. "We can, but we can't afford for the militia to waste themselves. Evacuate New Eden."

"Just hold. Trust me," Rick said.

"Will do," Jason answered.

"Think there's a chance he'll bring enough help?"

Jason shook his head. "I don't see how. The militia got their asses handed to them in the raid. There's not enough left."

"So what's the plan?" Latham asked.

"Well….I'm too damn tired to run. We've got an hour. The mountain slopes are pretty steep right here."

"Uh…yeah? Your point?" Latham looked at Holliman, confused.

"Gentlemen? This is Thermopylae."

Holliman seemed to consider it for a few moments before nodding.

Latham, in contrast, seemed to understand immediately. He smiled broadly. "Not a bad way to go, is it?"

"Not quite what I want, but hell…I never thought I'd last this long."

Mark Hernandez walked up. "Anyone need ammo?"

Jason nodded. The other man began handing him magazines. Hernandez was one of many ammo runners right now, always ducking just beyond the enemy's sight to reload on ammo, then back into the fray.

"Finish passing out what you've got," Jason said, "then head into New Eden. Understood?"

Mark shook his head. "I can't do that. I just can't."

"You've got a family in there."

Mark looked at him defiantly. "So do you."

True enough, but still…

"Doesn't matter. I'm passing the same order for all the ammo runners. Just get all the ammo passed around within the next forty-five minutes, then bug the hell out." Jason rubbed his weary eyes.

Hernandez looked at the three men. "Why?"

Jason took a deep breath. He needed to find the right words. "Because this is it, Mark. This is it. Welcome to the Alamo. Welcome to Bastogne." Jason realized he'd been speaking louder than he meant to, fatigue screwing up his judgment. A crowd began to form around them. *Ah, shit.*

"Beyond here?" he said, his voice now intentionally loud enough. "Beyond here are farms. Small homesteads that consider themselves part of New Eden. Beyond that is the town itself. A few thousand people who wanted nothing more than to be left alone. But that wasn't good enough for Conklin.

"He thought he could just take what he wanted. So he took Mark and his family. He took fifteen of our people for God knows what. He started a fight that we didn't want.

"Well, we're fighting now. My son says help is on the way. We just have to hold out. Can we? Who the hell knows. What I do know is that I'm not about to just roll over and let those people who live past this point find themselves at the tender mercies of Terry Conklin and his people.

"He's hurt too many people. Here we hurt him. Now, we make him feel all the pain he's inflicted on others. *This,*" Jason said, drawing a line in the soft Tennessee soil, "is the line in the sand. It's not proverbial anymore. It's literal, and he will not set one foot across this line so long as I draw a single breath."

Jason looked around. Fear seemed to grip the souls of many of the men. He could certainly understand why, but he meant what he'd said. He knew there was more to say though.

"Look, I know you're scared. You'd have to be an idiot not to be. But this is the kind of thing that becomes legend. Terry Conklin and his regime *will* fall. He *will* answer for his crimes. When he does, people for ages on will look to this day. 'That was the day,' they'll say, 'when brave men stood against a monster.' In their mind, we all would have died here. They're wrong.

"No, we'll live on. As long as someone remembers us, we will live on. Long after Terry Conklin is burning in Hell, we'll live on. He'll become a symbol of all that is wrong with this new world we live in. Us though? We will be immortal!" Jason finished, expecting triumphant applause. Instead, he was met with silence.

Not quite the response I had in mind. I mean, it was cheesy as hell, but still... Internally, he cringed. It hadn't been enough. He'd probably gone overboard on that last line, but it seemed like the thing to do. New Eden was dead, and it was because he couldn't rally the troops.

A moment later, a head nodded. Then another, and another. More and more joined in, then someone began clapping. That too was taken up en mass.

Jason exhaled in relief.

The men stopped their applause and shouts. "Alright," Jason said, "We've got less than an hour before that son of a bitch is at our door steps. Get to work. We can rest when all this is over."

The men dispersed and got to work. Jason turned to look around. Holliman stared back at him, a goofy smile on his face. "What?" Jason asked.

"You actually believe that shit?"

He shrugged. "More or less."

"Oh?"

"Well, I believe we're going to die here, so there's that."

Holliman nodded. "But we'll be immortal?"

"What? If they're dead, they'll never know if I'm right or not, now will they?"

Holliman nodded. "So now what?"

"Well, we're going to park our asses right here, and we're not going to move."

"So, you're sticking with that plan?"

"It worked for Leonidas," Jason quipped.

Latham shrugged. "Not really. Remember, he didn't make it. Despite what I said earlier, I'd really rather not die today."

"Yeah, but he accomplished his goal," he said. He cut his eyes to the ground and slowly shook his head. "The truth is, I'm spent. I don't have anything better. I'm open to suggestions." He looked at the two men, hopeful.

The two exchanged glances, then slowly shook their heads.

"I've got jack," Latham said.

"Same here," answered Holliman.

"Okay, then the plan is to stay put. We're a stone wall. Just one thing."

"Yeah?" Holliman asked.

"Don't get shot." Jason smiled.

"Sounds like a plan, then," Latham joked.

** ** **

The preparations had all been made. Latham's mad bomber had rigged some surprises to cover their flanks. Jason didn't know how much dynamite the man had carried but he'd already blown up a few of Conklin's men as it was. The only stipulation he'd given the man this time was to use it all.

Latham checked his watch. Conklin's men should be there soon. Jason had scouts out front to keep an eye out just to be sure.

"How much longer?" Jason asked.

"Well, if they're trying to be punctual, about ten minutes," he asked.

"Somehow, I suspect they won't be. So rude," Jason said.

Latham nodded. "No manners anymore. That's the problem with people these days."

"I swear, it's enough to make a man violent."

"Tsk, tsk. You know, violence isn't the answer."

Jason smiled. "I know. I'm going to get that question wrong on purpose."

"Coming in," someone down the line shouted.

Jason focused down range. Two men ran toward them at an all out sprint. He recognized them as the two forward scouts.

"They're comin'," the scout said, jumping over their cover and sliding to a stop. "A whole pile of 'em."

"How far?"

The man shook his head. "A whole lot closer than I'd like 'em to be. Probably just a few minutes."

Jason nodded and sent the men back to their unit.

"You know," Latham said, "it's so nice to

deal with gentlemen these days. I mean, sure he's a sick, sadistic bastard tyrant, but at least he isn't uncouth."

"Of course. It's the little things, don't you think?" Jason couldn't help but picture Jess, shaking her head at the conversation, her red hair swinging behind her, but a smile stretched across her face. Unfortunately, the bastard responsible for her not being around was coming.

Jason rested his rifle on the fallen tree. Considering the little time they had, and how tired everyone was, they'd put together a respectable fighting position. Hasty foxholes, supported by logs, formed the first line of defense. Directly behind them were larger logs that served as cover for the second line. Small gaps had been left between the logs to pull the wounded back.

The ammo runners were gone. Mark Hernandez didn't like it, and Jason could respect that. The man might not be a fighter in his core, but he damn sure wasn't a coward either. For a decade, he'd been convinced there were only two kinds of people. Hernandez showed him just how wrong he'd been.

The first black uniform wove through the trees. *Probably scouts. At least, that's what I'd do.*

Jason aimed and fired twice, both rounds

hitting the scout.

Around him, men looked at him in surprise. "What?" he asked as he looked at the incredulously. "Did you *really* think he wasn't going to find us?"

A round of nervous laughter broke out.

"Alright, everyone. Hold your fire until I give the order. Take aim, shoot to kill, all that stuff." He looked around. "Gentlemen, it's been a pleasure."

A black suited soldier in a white flag approached. "I have orders to meet with Jason Calvin, if he's still alive."

"What do you want?" Jason called back.

"Mr. Calvin?"

"Yeah. So, what do you want?"

"It's traditional for you to meet in the middle of the field under a flag of truce."

"If Conklin ain't there, I'm not coming. You'll understand if I'm less than trusting of the asshole."

The man stood tall, apparently proud to wear that black uniform and apparently feeling insulted on his commander's behalf. "General Conklin asked me to tell you that this would be a hell of a time for a surrender."

Jason seemed to consider for a moment. "Tell the General he's right. We accept, but you're going to have to put your weapons down and march about two miles in the other direction."

"You know that's not what he's talking about," the messenger said, clearly getting aggravated.

"Yeah, I know, it's an old joke, but so is Conklin, so all of you black shirts can kiss my lily white ass!"

A round of whoops and catcalls met his declaration. Jason didn't like to admit it, but he was enjoying the attention.

The soldier turned and stormed off.

"I'd say he didn't like your words," Latham said.

Jason shrugged. "Why? I mean, they were all from the heart. That's got to count for something." He smiled. He knew he was hiding his fear behind false bravado, but the men around him didn't, and that might make a difference down the road.

The black shirts got closer. They were taking their time. Of course, there was no reason they should, either. As far as they knew, they had all the time in the world. Of course, Jason figured they did anyways.

Two hundred yards now, as best as he could tell. They were trying to stay off the roads, which wasn't surprising. They filed down the sparse forest that lined the abandoned highway.

For four days, they'd bled Conklin and his men, and now it all came down to this. One hundred fifty yards now. *Come on, you bastards. Just a little closer.*

Jason selected his target and rested his sites on the man as he moved through the trees. One hundred twenty-five yards, and moving closer. Jason focused on his breathing.

One hundred yards. *Say goodnight, asshole.* Jason squeezed the trigger. The man dropped a split second later.

The woods erupted once again as the shooting ripped through the brush and brambles.

Chapter 19

Conklin was beyond sick of this crap. His troops had been eaten alive for four days. Morale was non-existent. Supplies were getting low, though more should be coming any time now - he was damned pissed at the delay.

Now, Calvin's troops looked like they were dug in between two fairly steep slopes. For half a hour, they'd thrown men at them, trying to pry them out.

Previous patterns said they'd have pulled back by now, but that wasn't happening. Conklin looked at the map unfolded on the ground in front of where he knelt. *We're getting close to home.*

As furious as Conklin was, he also recognized that he'd finally found someone who could give him a fight. He'd always wanted a challenge on the battlefield, but there wasn't one. Nowhere he'd been, none of the would-be warlords he'd crushed, none of them could give him a challenge.

Now, right in front of him was the first worthy adversary he'd ever had. Part of him knew he should have been thankful. Instead, he was just pissed and wanted to crucify this man.

Conklin took a deep breath. He recognized the rage taking him over. It happened more and more these days, and he couldn't afford it. Command required a cool head. *If only I had that little bitch still. I'd be feeling a whole lot better.*

He looked at the map, and old topographical map of the region. He looked to the two men with him. "Barry, take your unit up and try and hit their left flank. Steve, you take the right."

Both men acknowledged their orders and went off to carry them out.

Conklin tried to see if they were having any impact on Calvin's lines. He stood up, pulled out his binoculars, and looked. Nothing. The trees that provided cover to Calvin's men also made it nearly impossible to see any dead or wounded.

Trails of his own men, wounded by the deadly fire. Many others were stacked to the side. *Damn son of a bitch is bleeding us to death. Too bad for him I've got a lot more blood to lose.*

For all that the Army taught him, they'd been wrong about men. They were a resource, renewable and expendable. He didn't mind dead men. What he minded was that he wasn't already through their line and on the way to that town.

Really could have used those mortars, he thought,

then immediately regretted it as the rage threatened to explode once again.

"Where the hell is Ramirez?" he asked. He hadn't seen his second in command for some time. All around him, men shrugged or shook their head. No one had a clue where he was.

Suddenly, the ground shook as a massive explosion rocked the area, followed by the echoing legion of trees collapsing. Conklin immediately looked toward the noise. It was one of the slopes beside the road.

Moments later, another explosion came from the opposite slope.

"Son of a bitch!" he screamed. "Will someone get me that worthless son of a bitch's head?"

** ** **

"How long?" Jason asked.

"Hour and a half," Latham replied.

Jason nodded, then keyed the throat mic. "Eden One to Eden Two."

Silence.

"Well, so much for that," he muttered. Then, into the throat mic again, "Eden One to Eden Two."

"Eden Two, go ahead."

"I hope to God you guys are getting close. There aren't a whole lot of us left."

"Copy that. We're making best time. Don't worry, Pop. We'll be there."

"I just hope I am," he said, then turned his attention toward the onslaught. Another explosion erupted on the side of the mountain. They'd all grown used to those. At least a dozen more since the first pair went off. The plan had worked though. Their flank hadn't been touched.

He aimed and fired, dropping another soldier. He didn't know how much longer they'd last. Based on the estimate from before the battle, Rick would be here in half an hour. Unfortunately, they'd gone from almost two hundred men to just seventy-five still combat effective. They were holding, but damned if he knew how.

"So…um…any plans?" Latham asked, a hopeful tone in his voice.

"Well, I'm not sure that the whole 'not dying' thing is going to be really practical right now."

"Well shit. I made an appointment for a pedicure," Latham said as he fired. Jason saw the impact on the black shirt's face, dropping him immediately.

Jason began firing, letting his subconscious

do most of the heavy lifting. He picked a target, he fired at the target. Time and time again, he found himself thanking his father's ghost for all those hours at the range. Luckily, he'd loved it. Still, his father demanded perfection with his technique, and it was saving his life right now.

This battle wasn't a chess match. The last four days might have been to some extent, but not this. This was a slugfest. The only hope they had was either. to make Conklin bleed more than he was willing to, or pray for a miracle.

"Eden Two to Eden One."

Jason steadied himself for bad news. Hope for the best, prepare for the worst, all that jazz. "Go ahead," he said.

"Tell your boys to keep your heads down."

Jason keyed the mic, ready to ask why. Before the words could escape his mouth, he heard thunder behind him. The sky was as blue as could be.

His eyes shot wide in sudden realization. "EVERYONE DOWN!" he shouted, then dropped behind the log an instant before the pounding hoofs came into view.

The newly arrived cavalry leapt over their fighting position, whooping and hollering. Gunfire blasted from the horde now charging Conklin's position.

The flood of horses finally gave way toward

a mass of infantry flowing out of the same trees. A familiar man walked up to him, calmly.

"Told you we'd be here," Rick said, holding his hand down.

Jason smiled. "You could have clued me in on the surprise." He took the offered hand and stood up.

He turned and surveyed the battlefield. Conklin's men had turned in and run.

"Don't worry," Rick said. "They won't get far."

"Oh?"

The younger man nodded. "We've got cavalry on the move to cut them off. Too bad the bastard is all infantry right now."

Jason smiled, wearily.

"Come on," Rick said. "Let's get your guys heading back toward town."

Shaking his head, Jason said, "No. Not yet."

Rick nodded.

Chapter 20

Lines of black shirted men walked single file, their hands on their heads. Surrounding them were men in an odd mix of clothing, nothing matching except their demeanor.

"So," Jason said, "you want to clue me in on what the hell happened?"

"It was Sully's idea. While we were gone, they reached out to the other settlements. Told them about you, what all happened, all that. Said we needed to unite against this new threat, yadda yadda yadda."

"And it worked?"

Rick looked around, then back at his father. "Obviously."

"A onetime alliance?"

The younger man shook his head. "Probably not. Simon apparently pointed out to them that people like Conklin were out there, and uniting together as one entity gave us a much better chance at fighting them off. Pretty much everyone else agreed, so welcome to the all new TVA."

"Really?"

"The Tennessee Valley Alliance."

"Well, that's better than what I thought you

were going to say. Never been real good with authority."

"Runs in the family."

Jason laughed briefly, then looked around at all the dead and wounded. Doctors and other trained personnel were rendering aid where they could, though many were beyond help. Many on both sides.

"Damn shame we keep having to do this kind of thing."

Rick nodded.

"Why don't we find the son of a bitch responsible?"

"Sounds like a fantastic idea," Rick said, a feral grin taking shape.

The two men found Terry Conklin sitting on the ground, his legs crossed in front of him, his hands tied behind his back.

Al Holliman stood in front of his former commander, his arms crossed as the man railed against him. "You're a damn traitor, you know that? You really think you're going to get away with this?"

"Actually," Rick said as they walked closer, "they did."

Conklin craned his neck around, trying to look at the younger man.

"What's the word?" Holliman asked.

"Milton's been on the horn with Somerton.

The resistance's plan actually worked. Most places at least. Somerton is completely in their hands. So are most other towns"

"Impossible!" Conklin barked.

"Where's Ramirez," Jason asked.

Holliman shook his head. "Best we can tell, he took some people loyal to him and bolted. I guess he didn't like this piece of shit too much either."

Conklin laughed. "He's loyal to me. He'll get me, and then we'll start laying waste to your little project here."

Jason and Rick pulled their side arms simultaneously, leveling the weapons at Conklin's face. "No, you won't," Jason said.

A half dozen people had assembled around Conklin. They all took a step back.

"What...? You can't!" Conklin stammered, his eyes wide, the pupils dilated until they looked black.

"We can't what? Kill you? Why the hell not?" Jason asked.

"After all, you targeted our home. Killed my mother. Could have killed my little sister. Did you even care?"

"But...collateral damage. It happens in war!"

Jason laughed. "War? Is that really the way you want to go with this? You attacked us. We responded, but there were no declarations of war. You know that. You murdered innocent people, and now you're trying to get out of it by saying it happens in war?"

He lowered his weapon. Jason said, "I'm not going to kill you."

Relief flooded Conklin's face.

"Oh, I wouldn't get too excited if I were you. You see, Somerton probably has a list of charges a mile long for you. Scott?"

Scott Latham nodded. "I'm partial to starting with the murder of Mindy Latham"

"Ouch," Jason said. "And I'm willing to bet that the good people of Somerton are likely to be fans of capital punishment."

Latham nodded.

"So, you see, you're a dead man either way," Jason said. He turned and saw that Rick's pistol was still pointed at the man. "Rick…"

"I want this piece of shit dead," the younger man whispered.

Jason nodded. "I know. I do too. But, I think Reverend Hardesty might have been right. This isn't the way to do it."

"I don't care."

"Then how about for Somerton?"

Rick glanced at his father for a moment, then back at Conklin. "What?"

"They need him. They *need* to try him. They

need to convict him. Otherwise, there's always going to be an emptiness in them."

"They going to try him for Mom? Huh?" Rick said, his voice rising.

"Yes," Latham answered. "He will be. He'll be tried for a lot of dead people. He's got a lot of blood on his hands."

Rick nodded. Slowly, the pistol lowered. As he holstered the weapon, Rick leaned forward. "You'd better *hope* they execute you. You see, they'll be quick. If you walk? I won't be."

Jason smiled at the condemned man. "One thing I raised my kid to be is honest. I'd bet on it if I were you."

Rick swung his weapon up in an instant, the report of his Glock as deafening as it was sudden. Conklin cried out in pain, his legs bleeding profusely.

The younger man looked around at the stunned crowd. "What? I didn't say I was going to make it easy to try and get away, now did I?"

** ** **

Jason slapped another hunk of mud against the form. His new home was taking shape. They'd opted to keep the same footprint, but the shape was a bit different. The odd domes were difficult to achieve, and he need a roof over his head as quickly as possible.

A dozen people followed his lead, slapping mud on the form. The rough walls were done, and now it was just a matter of prettying the house up a bit.

It wasn't the house he and Jess had shared, but he wondered if that was for the best. She'd been dead for several months, but it still felt like yesterday to him. He suspected it would for some time, but that was alright.

Rick walked through the vacant doorway, building a door one of a million other things he had left to do.

"So," Jason said, "you hear yet?"

His son smiled and nodded.

"You're in?"

"You're looking at the newest TVA Ranger."

"Alright!" Jason exclaimed. The new Ranger service was a hybrid law enforcement agency for the area between towns and military cadre. The perfect place for a hardened veteran like him.

"Where are they basing you out of?" he asked.

Rick pointed to the ground. "Here, believe it or not."

Jason smiled. "Great! You tell Katie yet?"

Rick's smile faded. "Uh...not yet."

"Problem?"

The younger man shrugged. "Maybe. Um...there's something I need to ask her. I'm kind of nervous."

Jason's smiled broadened. "Just ask. It'll be fine."

"So..." Rick said, looking around at all the busy people, "how much longer you have on this place?"

He shrugged. "Not sure. It's probably going to get delayed a bit though. Need to head to Somerton for the trial."

Rick nodded. "Spectator, or witness."

He shrugged. "Bit of both, maybe? They want me as a witness, but part of me wants to watch the son of a bitch hang."

"I guess I can understand that."

Jason jerked his head toward the door, a request to get his son to follow him.

They stepped out of the muddy cylinder, which is all the house really was at this point, and onto the grass.

"Any word about that idea to bring women into the militia? That go out the window?"

Rick shook his head. "Nope. That's still happening. A pile of them going through the training right now. Including Katie."

"Now *that* doesn't surprise me in the least." Jason paused for a moment. "You're sure about this Ranger thing?" he asked, his tone more somber.

"I thought you were happy about it," Rick asked, a confused look on his face.

Jason smiled, trying to take the sting out of his question. "I am. Don't get me wrong there. I just want to make sure you want it for the right reasons."

Rick shrugged. "For better or worse? All that shit we went through? It's the only time in my life that I felt like I was doing what I should have been doing."

"The switch."

Rick nodded.

"Fair enough. There is something I wanted to ask you though."

"Shoot." Rick smiled. Jason realized he wasn't talking like a guy calling the shots, or a parent, but man to man. Despite his age, that's exactly what his son was. A man.

"You know how I always said there were two kinds of people left in this world? Fighters and cowards?"

Rick nodded.

"You knew I was wrong, didn't you?"

"Not really. I'm still not sure you're wrong."

"Mark Hernandez is pretty clear proof I was wrong," Jason said, a smug look on his face. He tried not to think of the irony of a smug look on his face about being wrong.

"Were you? Stayed with you guys, ran through gunfire while unarmed, knowing he was going to share your fate. Didn't you say he was ready to stay with you 'til the end?"

Jason nodded.

"Sounds like a fighter to me."

"Where the hell did you get the Wisdom of Solomon from? Huh?" Jason said with a smile, his arm closing around his son's neck.

"Oh, that's easy. I got it from Mom," Rick said, smiling as well.

** ** **

Justin Ramirez wasn't looking forward to this as he wove his way through the crowd and cigarette smoke so thick he almost needed a machete to hack his way through as pounding music blasted into his ears.

Two large men stood outside the door, their tattooed arms crossed.

"I need to see him," Ramirez said.

The man on the right knocked on the door.

The battered wooden door, decade's worth of band stickers forming a quilt work of rock and roll history, opened just crack. "Yes?" a squeaky voice called, barely loud enough to be heard over the music. Only a beady eye could be seen through the tiny chink.

"I need to see him," Ramirez repeated.

"Wait here," the voice said, closing the door immediately.

Long moments passed before the door opened. The beady eyed man stood before him, shirtless and covered in tattoos as well. "Right this way," the man said, turning and walking away without waiting to see if he was being followed.

Ramirez nodded and followed. The room was filled with women, some barely clothed...and they looked overdressed for the occasion. Stacks of white powder, sealed beneath clear plastic film and duct tape lined one wall from floor to ceiling.

His guide lead him past that and into a small room, empty except for a small desk, two chairs and a man with piercing blue eyes and jet black hair. He was also shirtless, but whereas the beady eyed man was scrawny, this man was built like a UFC fighter. Powerful muscles competed with nothing as there didn't seem to be an ounce of body fat anywhere on the man.

"Mr. Declan," Ramirez said.

"What do you want?" the man with the blue eyes asked.

"He's been taken."

The man studied him for a moment, then

nodded. "How?"

"He picked a fight with a town called New Eden. They had a lot more fight than he thought they would."

"Terry always did like to bite off more than he could chew."

Ramirez nodded.

"He dead?"

"Not yet. He's on trial right now, but he's guilty as hell. They'll convict him, and they'll execute him."

The man nodded. "Well then. Sounds like I need to pay this New Eden a little visit."

Ramirez nodded again.

"I take it you need a job?" the man asked.

"Me and some of my men could use one, yes sir."

"Don't worry. You did right by me. I'll do right by you."

Ramirez breathed easier. "Yes, sir."

About the Author

T.L. Knighton began his love affair with science fiction in a dark movie theater in 1977. That was when he saw the opening scene to the original Star Wars. A ship crossing the screen, laser blasts rocking it. He was hooked.

He wrote off and on since early elementary school. As an adult, he proudly served as a Hospital Corpsman in the United States Navy. Honorably discharged in 1996, he returned to his home town of Albany, Georgia where he currently lives with his wife, two children, and two former deities who do not understand why people no longer worship them as they so richly deserve (commonly known as "cats").

Visit T.L. at his website, http://tlknighton.com or his Facebook page, http://www.facebook.com/TLKnighton.